D1230183

BUSTER ADAMS
AND THE
RAGAMUFFIN GANG

BUSTER ADAMS AND THE RAGAMUFFIN GANG

•

KENT CONWELL

AVALON BOOKS
THOMAS BOUREGY AND COMPANY, INC.
401 LAFAYETTE STREET
NEW YORK, NEW YORK 10003

PRINTED IN THE UNITED STATES OF AMERICA
ON ACID-FREE PAPER
BY HADDON CRAFTSMEN, SCRANTON, PENNSYLVANIA

To Susan,
who grew up overnight

Chapter One

I had been riding the San Antone-El Paso road for several days when I spotted the Great Comanche War Trail ahead, a mile wide and littered with bones as far to the north and south as the eye could see.

Despite the stifling heat and choking dust, I grinned. Five more days now, and I'd reach San Antone, with one day to spare. Five more days and I would be well on my way to being a man of substance, a man Natalia Ludden's father would be forced to respect, a man who could ask for Natalia's hand in marriage with pride.

I cut across the prairie, angling for the spot where the war trail intersected the Pecos River at Horsehead Crossing. I pulled up on the bluff overlooking the river and froze. Below, swimming in the cool waters of the river were two young women, one about twelve, the other around twenty, each wearing some sort of white shift.

My mouth dropped open, and I stared like a lovesick boy. I hadn't seen a woman in a month; triple that time since I'd seen a pretty one.

My mustang, Hey, stood motionless, his head cocked to one side, watching the young women just like I was. I wasn't really thinking about where they came from or who might be with them. All I knew was that I wanted to get a closer look, so I dismounted and started down the steep bluff.

The trail down to the river led past a thick clump of mesquite. Normally, I'm doubly alert in Indian country, but the unexpected sight before me sort of dulled my senses. I sneaked past the mesquite and the next thing I knew, a flying tangle of arms, legs, feathers, fur, flapping wings, and snapping teeth struck me and sent me tumbling into the river below.

I hit the cold water, my arms and legs windmilling in an effort to throw off whatever had landed on me. When the water closed about my head, I kicked hard toward the middle of the river.

When I poked my head up, one woman, five children, one dog, and a hissing goose were standing ankle deep in water glaring at me. The oldest boy held a Sharps carbine lined up on my forehead, the hammer cocked.

His voice cracked when he spoke. "Just you take it easy, mister. You don't give us no trouble, and you won't get yourself hurt none." Behind him, a mangy black dog barked.

Here I was, in the middle of the river, treading water, about to drown, and he thought I was going to give *them* trouble? I shook my head and spit out a mouthful of water. "Don't worry about me, boy. I don't plan on causing anybody any trouble." I eased toward the shore.

The goose flapped her wings, hissed, and came bouncing across the water at me. I splashed water at her, driving her away. She honked angrily, and skirted around me, twisting her neck and darting her head at me.

I took a stroke toward the shore.

"Hold it right there." I glanced up as the young boy tilted the muzzle of the Sharps. "I told you to just stay where you are, mister." He glanced at the young woman who had come to stand by his side. "We ain't decided what we're goin' to do with you."

By now, my arms and legs were getting heavy. My boots felt like they weighed fifty pounds, and the Colts on my hips another fifty pounds. I was accustomed to forking ponies, not treading water. My strength was fast running out. "You better decide something fast, boy. I'm coming in. Else, I'll drown, or this duck out here will poke my eyes out."

I started in, slow, my eyes fixed on the boy with the Sharps. He glanced uncertainly at the young woman who nodded at the shoreline. Together, they all backed onto the bank, and I followed while the goose remained in the rear, paddling in a small circle in the river, hissing and honking.

When my feet touched bottom, I halted, not wanting to frighten them, especially the boy with the Sharps. I didn't know how good a shot he was, but that carbine appeared to be about a 50-70, powerful enough to do a heap of damage no matter where it hit a jasper.

Holding up my hands, I said, "Name's Buster Adams. Just passing through . . . heading to San Antone."

The mangy dog yapped a couple times as the young woman took a step forward, a pair of trousers draped around her shoulders. Her black hair clung to her head, and water beaded on her dark face. "What are you spying on us for?"

I shook my head. "You got me wrong, lady. I wasn't spying on you."

Her black eyes flashed, and her lips bared her even white teeth. "It sure looked that way to us, you sneaking down the bluff like a snake."

The boy with the Sharps pulled himself erect. Next to him were two boys and two girls, all younger. The two boys, both freckle-faced, nodded emphatically. "Yeah," said one. "We saw you."

"Yes," one of the girls volunteered.

The black dog continued his incessant yapping. One of the boys with freckles laid his hand on the dog's head. "Be quiet, Dog. Yeah, we saw you," he said.

I tried to explain. "All I did was ride up and . . ."

"And spy," said the older boy, giving the Sharps a threatening jab at me.

Usually, I'm a patient man, but now I was growing tired of standing chest deep in the river, hounded by a sloughful of children and a yapping dog, with the crazy name of Dog, in front and a honking goose behind. I glanced around for a man, but saw none, not even by the freight wagon on the far shore, so I turned back to the young woman. "Ma'am, I mean no harm, but I'm coming out of the water. Then I'm climbing that bluff behind you, getting on my pony, and riding out of here."

"D—Don't you move," sputtered the young boy with the Sharps.

The muzzle wobbled. The boy stepped back as I waded ashore.

I won't lie and tell you I wasn't worried, because I was, mighty worried. A cannon that size in the hands of a scared boy—I didn't even want to think about the kind of damage he could do.

Pausing in front of the boy, I nodded to the top of the bluff. "That's where I'm going."

He did what I thought he'd do and looked up. Quick as a striking snake, I grabbed the big Sharps and yanked it from him, ducking at the same time. He yelled and jumped back, inadvertently pulling the trigger. The big saddlegun roared, almost deafening me.

Squealing like frightened rabbits, the children all huddled together, except for the young woman. She stood in front of them, facing me with her jaw set, her fists clenched. The dog stood silently, panting hard, its tongue hanging out.

I ejected the spent shell from the chamber. "I told you I meant no harm, and I don't. I was surprised to see anyone in this part of the state, especially someone swimming in the river." I handed her both the empty brass and the Sharps. "I won't bother you no more," I added, climbing the bluff to my pony.

At the top of the bluff, I looked around for her man again, knowing I shouldn't leave her and the kids out here by themselves, yet not wanting to waste more time. San Antone was still five days away.

After I swung up on Hey, I nodded to her and touched my fingers to the brim of my hat. I urged the pony down the incline to the river, still wondering where her man was. There was no sign of him up river or down.

She stopped me before I entered the water. "Please, Mr. Adams."

I reined up.

"I apologize for our behavior," she said. "It was just that you frightened us."

"Well," I replied, nodding to the Sharps. "You scared me too."

For the first time, a faint grin played over her lips. "Please, it's getting late. Won't you take a meal with us before you ride on? It's the least we can do."

Before I could reply, she continued. "I'm Elena Wallace." She hesitated and gestured to the children. "These . . . These are my . . . my children." She introduced them, but so fast I didn't remember any names except the young man who had pointed the Sharps at me, Robert Chapman. "To make up for our poor manners, we'd be happy for you to stay for supper," she added.

I hadn't put myself around anything solid since I left Mesilla up in New Mexico Territory a few days before, and my belly had come to the conclusion that my mouth had been nailed shut. The prospect of a hot meal was too much to pass up. "Where's your man?"

The faint smile fled her face. "Oh, h—he's out scouting ahead. He'll be back directly."

She was lying. It was plain as the button nose on her face, but I didn't let on. What she was up to was her business. I'd just make it a point to look after my back. "Well, Ma'am. Dinner sounds mighty fine if it won't be too much trouble."

She glanced at the children. "Come on, children. Let's get back to the wagon."

They all swam the river and, with practiced hands,

set up the evening camp, the boys laying a small fire and tending the six draft horses while the two girls, Rachel and Mary, prepared the meal, one sliding the heavy pots into the coals while the other dug out the grub. The now-silent goose fluttered its wings and squatted nearby where she could keep an eye on Rachel.

I looked around the camp. I was growing more and more confused.

After a meal of corn dodgers, boiled succotash, and fresh coffee, I leaned back and studied the small party I had fallen in amongst. Five children and a young woman.

The two redheads were the Taylor brothers, Bernard and George; the second set of siblings was the Chapmans, Bob and Mary, both with straight black hair and brooding eyes. Mary was the silent one. Then there was the talkative little blonde girl with the goose, Rachel Sheridan, about eight, I guessed.

My eyes settled on the young woman, Elena, who wore a plain white blouse and a pair of riding pants tucked into boottops with fancy stitching. "That was right tasty, Ma'am."

By now, the sun had dropped below the mountains to the west, random clouds carving dark slashes in the pink glow of the sunset.

I stared into the encroaching darkness. "Your man's been out there a long time."

She shifted nervously on the drift log on which she sat. "He . . . He'll be back. Don't worry," she replied, her voice quivered with bravado. There was a certain tightness about her, a tension like when you're waiting for the other shoe to fall. She seemed to be waiting for something.

About the only fact I knew for sure was she did have a man with her, or at least a man had been with them earlier, for when I tied Hey to the wagon, I spotted boot tracks leading east into the cactus- and mesquite-studded prairie. But where was he now?

None of the children spoke a word, but as the night grew darker, they pulled in closer to the small fire, casting worried glances into the darkness surrounding them. Except for one, a red-headed youngster who was fascinated by my twin Colts. Still, tension mounted.

Elena broke the taut silence. "You say you're headed to San Antonio, Mr. Adams?"

"Yep." I leaned back on my elbows and studied the flames at my feet. The fire was small, and down in an arroyo, so its glow couldn't be spotted unless someone drew too close. "Meeting a friend to drive some cattle to Abilene."

"I see."

She lapsed into silence. The boy with the Sharps sat with his back against the wheel of the big freight wagon, which was another puzzlement. Why were they riding in one of those big, lumbering freight wagons?

Why not a smaller, easier handled Conestoga? More to the point, what were they doing out here, a man, a woman and three different sets of kids? I tried to shrug off the questions. It was none of my business, but their predicament nagged at me.

Out on the prairie, a cricket chirped, and a rabbit squealed. I nodded to the children. "Your kin, Mrs. Wallace?"

She glanced over her shoulder, the firelight illuminating her face. Her cheeks darkened with a blush. "No. It's Miss Wallace, not Mrs." Her gaze darted to my side. "Bernie! No. Leave Mr. Adams' sixguns alone."

I glanced down to see the young red-headed boy jerk his finger away. Before I could say anything, the other redhead stood up and crooked his finger at Bernie. "I got to go." He nodded to the darkness.

Bernie snorted. "Go by yourself, George. You ain't no baby."

George's bottom lip quivered. He looked at me and struggled to hold back the tears. Elena broke in. "Go on, Bernie. George *is* your little brother. Go with him."

Bernie gave a last wistful look at the Colt on my hip and with a resigned sigh, rose and accompanied his brother into the darkness. Dog rose and trotted beside the boy.

Rachel and Mary had come to sit on either side of

Elena, leaning against the log and resting their heads on her knees. She smiled down at them, a fragile, almost sad smile, and gently laid her slender fingers on their heads.

I glanced into the darkness surrounding us, hoping her man would return. I didn't want to ride out and leave them alone, but they hadn't invited me to stay. Besides, I reminded myself, with the waning moon rising in the next hour or so, I could make another fifteen or twenty miles. Lorenzo Scott and those longhorns wouldn't wait in San Antone for me, children or not.

Rising to my feet, I snugged my hat down on my head. "Much obliged to you, Miss Wallace. Reckon I'll be pushing on."

She stiffened, then quickly relaxed. "If . . . If you wish, Mr. Adams. Of course, you're more than welcome to throw your bedroll by the fire," she said, a little more urgently than she intended. "If—that is— if you want."

I nodded to her, relieved that she had offered the invitation, but on the other hand, impatient to get on with my own journey. "That'd be right nice, Miss Wallace." I cleared my throat and nodded to the darkness. "No offense intended, but I'd feel right uncomfortable bedding down without your man agreeing."

Her eyes flashed in the firelight. "He won't mind, Mr. Adams. You can rest assured of that."

Something in her tone told me she was right. "Thanks for the offer, Ma'am. Then I'd suggest that everyone hit the blankets so we can put out the fire. No sense in showing ourselves to any wandering Indians. The glow lights up the sky when it's real dark."

She seemed to relax then, the tension draining away. I wanted to ask her more, but she disappeared into the wagon. I kept waiting for her man to reappear. When he didn't, I pulled the blankets over my shoulder and tried to push aside my curiosity over her and those children out here by themselves.

But I couldn't. They were in danger out here all by their lonesomes. And suddenly, I was faced with a dilemma. What if something happened to her man? What if he didn't return? Then what would I do? I muttered an oath at my ability to always find myself in some sort of quandry.

The next morning, I rose before false dawn. Gently, I shook the older boy awake and motioned him to follow me a distance away from the wagon. "What's your name, son?"

He gripped the Sharps and eyed me suspiciously. "Robert. But they call me Bob."

"Okay, Bob. I got to get on to San Antone, but I don't want to see you all out here by your lonesomes. This man who was with you. Where is he? He's been out all night."

Bob cut his eyes to the wagon where the girls were

sleeping. "I told her not to take him on. He's some bullwhacker who escaped from the Mescaleros. We found him on the trail after we left the ranch."

"What ranch?"

"The one we all lived on. Apaches killed ever'one. We was on a picnic with Elena. Her pa was manager. Mine and Mary's was foreman. When we got back, they was all dead, so we buried them and loaded up the wagon and headed for San Antone, just like you. We had to go around Fort Davis and Fort Stockton. The bullwhacker claimed they was surrounded by Mescaleros."

I looked back at the wagon. So that was what it was all about. "This bullwhacker. Where'd he go?"

Bob shrugged. "We run across a deserted ranch west of Fort Stockton. He found some whiskey. When we stopped here yesterday, he wandered off in the prairie with a bottle in each hand. Said he wanted to relax from the screeching of females and the yapping of runny-nosed children."

Blast!

I'd of bet a double eagle there was no Mescaleros around Fort Davis or Stockton. Chances were, the law was after that bullwhacker, and he dared not show his face.

The sun peeked over the eastern horizon. Normally, I enjoy sunrises, the soaking heat of the rising sun warming my muscles, but today, I felt cold all over.

I couldn't just ride away. Yet, their man would return. He could take care of them.

I grinned at Bob. "Let's get a fire going. Then we'll figure out our next step."

He stood fast, his jaw set, his eyes determined. "You don't have to stay here with us." He held up the Sharps. "I can take care of Elena—I mean, of us. I'm almost full growed."

He looked me square in the eye. I was only about five-six, and I knew exactly how he felt when folks gave you a look that laughed at you. "I'm not arguing, Bob. I know you can take care of them." I hooked my thumb toward the wagon. "Now, what about the fire?"

While coffee was boiling, I convinced myself that the best course was to be perfectly honest with them, see if we could find a solution that would work for us all. If I'd known then what I learned a few minutes later, I'd have kept my mouth shut and done what should have been done.

Elena Wallace stared at me over the fire, her fists jammed in her hips. "We don't need you here, Mr. Adams. So, don't worry about us. Ride on out. Our man will be back soon. He probably got drunk and is sleeping it off. Don't stay around for our sake. Far be it from us to ask you a favor."

"You don't understand," I hastened to explain, trying to salvage some semblance of civility out of our suddenly deteriorating relationship. "All I said was, I'd ride ahead to Fort Lancaster and send help back. I'll leave you my Winchester and extra cartridges. The cavalry will get here by morning."

She shook her head. Before she answered, I glanced at Bob and played my hole card. "Bob there can look after things just fine, can't you, son?

"In fact," I said, without giving Elena a chance to reply, "I found a cave overlooking the valley. It has a rocky entrance that will hide the wagon tracks. We'll wipe out the tracks in the sand. You'll be all right as long as you stay inside."

Bob Chapman looked at her hopefully. "We can do it, Elena. Honest, we can. I can look after us until the army gets here."

Elena did not answer him. She kept her black eyes fixed on mine. "We don't need your cave or your help, Mr. Adams. Like I said, our driver will be back." She set her jaw. "We put up with you last night because we felt sorry for you. The best thing you can do now is ride out of here. We got this far, we'll get the rest of the way without your help."

I held my temper, but it was sizzling like a pan full of bear grease. "Look, I don't want to leave, but if I don't reach San Antone in five days, I'll lose everything I've worked for, my ranch, my girl . . . everything. I can reach Fort Lancaster by tonight. A patrol will be back here tomorrow. If I stay with you, it's three days to the fort. There's no chance of me reaching San Antone in two more days from there.''

Her nostrils flared. Her eyes shot daggers. ''Then go. Get out of here. Leave us alone.'' She spun on her heel and stormed back to the fire.

I nodded to Bob. Together we set the horses in harness. As we hooked the wheelers up to the single-trees, I asked, ''You sure you can get the wagon up to the cave?''

''Yes.''

''And don't forget to wipe out the tracks in the sand.''

''Don't worry. I told you I was growed up. I can do the job as good as you.''

I glanced back at the fire. The other children sat staring at us. Elena busied herself about the fire, her back to me. For a moment, I weakened. How could I ride off and leave such a helpless lot? But, they made it from the Rio Grande to here, and that journey was just as dangerous as the one ahead.

Out here in the west, everyone took his chance. I grinned at Bob. ''Look after them, son.''

He snapped back at me. ''I ain't your son.''

His reply slapped me between the eyes. I stared at him, silently thanking the Lord that this smart-alec boy wasn't my son. I swung into the saddle, relieved to be shed of them despite the guilt sagging about my shoulders.

Squeezing my knees, I urged the little mustang up the side of the arroyo and onto the prairie, heading southeast for the fort. I didn't look back, fearful that one glance of one of those small girls or boys would make me change my mind.

"After all," I said to Hey, "this might be my last chance to amount to anything."

Normally, Hey would twitch an ear when I spoke to him, but this time, he gave no indication of hearing me.

The prairie between Horsehead Crossing and Fort Lancaster was covered with slashing arroyos. Ten minutes later, I found the bullwhacker, sprawled on the sandy bed of an arroyo. He had been scalped.

I muttered a curse and stared across the prairie in the direction of San Antone. Well, it had been a nice dream.

Chapter Two

Neither Elena nor the children had moved from where they sat clustered around the fire. The children grinned when I pulled up on the rim of the arroyo and looked down at them, all except Bob. He just glowered.

Elena tilted her chin, a habit I was beginning to dislike. "Did you forget something, Mr. Adams?" Her voice was cold enough to freeze the Pecos River.

I had learned the hard way that if a man has a disagreeable job, he jumps right in and starts chopping. Well, facing her and her menagerie of kids and animals had to be considered mighty disagreeable by any gent in his right mind.

Taking a deep breath, I pushed Hey down into the arroyo. "Yes, Ma'am, I did forget something."

"What?"

I dismounted and tied Hey to the tailgate. "You all," I replied, gesturing to the kids. "Now, let's load up. We don't have time to waste."

Elena started to protest, but I cut her off. "Your man is out there, dead and scalped. You bunch of helpless pilgrims won't get ten miles before you join him. I might not be much, but I'm not going off and leaving you." I kicked the fire out.

Bob Chapman spoke up. "I told you I could take care of us. We don't . . . "

I spun on him, my temper perched on the breaking point. "Look, boy. You do what I say, or I'll put my boot where it'll do the most good. You hear?"

He screamed and grabbed his arm as an arrow thudded into the wagon.

Behind him on the far rim of the arroyo, two Mescaleros stepped from behind some mesquite scrub, their bows drawn.

Like magic, my Colts leaped into my hand and boomed twice, before either warrior could release his arrow. The impact of the 250 grain slugs knocked them back. One fell on the rim, and the other tumbled down the slope to the bed of the arroyo in a cloud of dust and rocks.

I raced to the rim, fearful of what I might find, but there were no other Mescaleros to be seen. The two Indian ponies stamped nervously, their eyes wide.

Speaking gently, I tried to approach them, but before I could grab their bridles, they spooked and bolted, speeding across the prairie with their heads high and tails flying.

Returning to the wagon, I found Elena tending Bob, but the rest of the children were staring at me, their mouths gaping. I yelled at them. "You hear me? I said load up the wagon, and let's get out of here!"

They scattered like quail, bustling about, throwing gear in the bed of the wagon. The black dog got into the spirit of the time, dashing about their feet, yapping like he had good sense. The goose just squatted and stared at me.

I noticed one of the boys, the one named Bernie Taylor, just sit back while the others did his work. I snapped at him. "You too, boy. Get the gear loaded."

He folded his arms over his chest and glared at me.

"You want me to put my boot where you sit?"

He just stared at me, defying me.

I took a step in his direction, and he jumped to his feet.

Grinning to myself, I dragged both the Mescaleros around the bend in the arroyo and pulled down part of the bank on them, covering them good. When I finished, I went to see about the Chapman boy. "How's his arm?"

Elena nodded without looking up. "Just a flesh wound. Not bad."

The three-foot arrow lay on the ground. I picked it up and studied the iron head. Sometimes, Mescaleros dipped their arrows in horse dung to poison the wound, but this one looked all right.

I tossed it aside. "Let's go. Load'em up."

Without waiting for a reply, I untied Hey and swung into the saddle. That's when the goose decided to waddle down to the river and take a swim. Rachel went running after the bird.

Elena called after her. "Rachel! Come back!"

"I can't leave Sally," she cried, wading into the river.

Muttering a curse, the first of many I would utter in the coming days, I kneed Hey after the girl.

The goose was having itself a nice little swim in the middle of the river, blithely ignoring our entreaties to return to shore. Rachel stood waist deep in the water, pleading with Sally *to please come in. We have to leave. Be a sweet goose and please come in.*

For a fleeting moment, I thought about the Colts on my hip and how they would solve this problem. Of course, that action, sensible as it seemed to me, would probably create a worse problem. Instead, Hey and I joined in the swim, anxious to round up that goose before more Mescaleros dropped into our laps.

I once heard an old wrangler compare herding longhorns to herding cats. I had news for him. Herding cats is nothing to herding a goose.

Finally, Sally went ashore, not because of Hey or me, but I figure because she was tired, and she had her fill of swimming for the day. Rachel knelt and hugged Sally. Then, like two little girls, they both waddled back to the wagon, water dripping from each of their behinds.

The sun was approaching mid-morning, and we hadn't made ten feet. I shook my head. The sixty miles to Fort Lancaster seemed a mighty long distance, especially with a band of murderous Mescaleros running loose.

Elena drove the freight wagon, and I've got to admit, she handled the ribbons like an old-timer, her flat-brimmed hat pulled low over her eyes against the all-consuming sun. Bob sat on the seat by her side, his face pale, but his fist clutching the Sharps something fierce. The children rode in the back, shielded from the sun by the canvas top stretched over the oaken bows. Bernie Taylor, the lazy one, slept all curled up in a ball, while Mary Chapman wrote in a little book of some sort and never said a word. The wagon wheels cut deep in the soil, a peculiarity I didn't notice at the time.

Our route skirted the northern boundaries of the *despoblado*, a harsh and unforgiving land, bordered on the west by the road from Chihuahua to El Paso and on the south by Parras and Torregon.

I rode far and wide, scanning the far mountains and

surrounding prairie for any sign of Mescaleros. Most of the tribes had settled on reservations, although many of the warriors continued to live their old way of life. Highly mobile, the Mescaleros, as the Kiowa and Comanche, would travel a hundred miles, raid and murder, then dash into the *despoblado*, the uninhabited land, for refuge from pursuit.

Once or twice, I spotted a thin wisp of dust far to the rear, but the scorching prairie wind blew it away. Dust devils, I figured, but I kept my eyes open just the same.

Mid-afternoon, we pulled up in the spotty shade of a clump of mesquite, more for the horses' benefit than ours. The children jumped from the wagon and stretched their cramped legs.

"Don't go running off," I called to them, still in the saddle.

The younger of the red-headed boys was stroking the head of one of the draft horses. "Be careful around those animals, Bernie. Don't get hurt."

The frail boy glared at me, his fingers scratching underneath the horse's jaw. "I ain't Bernie. I'm George. That's Bernie. He's a year older than me," he said, pointing to the other redhead. "Besides, I ain't goin' to get hurt. My pa was a buster on the ranch. He showed me how to handle horses."

"I don't care. You get away from that animal.

Now.'' The boy took a tentative step backward. ''And leave them alone. I don't want you hurt.''

The way he glared at me, I knew I'd made another enemy. I shook my head, wishing the remaining miles to Fort Lancaster would pass quickly.

The other redhead climbed up in a mesquite and perched on a limb at eye level with me. Dog squatted on the ground beneath the boy. ''George is right, Mister. He's the best of us all with horses. Even if he is only a kid and my little brother. He's the best with horses. Why, I seen him walk into a corral and ever' last one of the horses would start tagging after him. They'd even stick their heads down so he could bridle them.''

I studied the youngster. Like his little brother, thin, frail almost to the point of being skin and bones, he was deadly serious. ''What's your name, boy?''

The youth glanced around, then turned back to me. ''Bernie. Bernie Taylor.''

''Well, now, Bernie,'' I began, a grin on my face. ''I reckon what you say about George might be right, but I just don't want to see him or none of you youngsters hurt. I don't mean to make him upset or nothing.'' I gestured to the wide open spaces around us. ''Out here, miles from help, is no place for someone to get hurt bad.''

Bernie shrugged. ''I understand, Mister. I just hope George does.''

Elena and the girls stood by the water barrel on the side of the wagon. The goose squatted beside Rachel, its beady eyes never leaving me.

I dismounted and started to the water barrel, but the goose jumped up and flapped its wings. Hissing like a rattlesnake, it made a couple of tentative charges at me. I backed up fast, holding my hand out, palm up. "Hold it, bird. I'm not going to hurt anyone."

Elena gave me a wry smile. "She's suspicious of strangers."

"How long does it take for a jasper not to be a stranger?"

She arched an eyebrow. Her smile broadened, but it was still not friendly. "Depends on the man."

Both girls climbed into the wagon. I looked at Elena. "It's been mighty tough on you, hasn't it?"

She stared up at me a moment, surprised at my remark. Her bottom lip quivered, and she ducked her head and dabbed a knuckle at her eyes. "Bob said he told you about the ranch." I nodded. She continued. "I didn't know what to do . . . where to go. Mescaleros kept us from Fort Davis and Fort Stockton, so I decided to head on to San Antonio. My pa has a brother there."

"He still there?"

She forced a weak grin. "I hope so."

Removing my hat, I ran my fingers through my hair. "Tough. On all of you."

A smile flickered across her lips. "We can manage." She was still defensive.

The remainder of the day passed without event. To the rear, I spotted a single tendril of dust, but it quickly blew away. For several minutes, I paused on a small mesa, studying our backtrail, but saw no indication of any pursuit. To the north, a dust devil bounced across the prairie.

Although we travelled until well after dark, we failed to make the miles I had hoped. The freight wagon, sixteen feet long and four and a half feet wide, was an original J. Murphy with red running gear and a blue box topped with white canvas.

Although solidly constructed with hickory axles, Osage orange wheel hubs, white oak spokes and wheel rims, and iron tires six inches wide and an inch thick, the wagon proved unduly cumbersome descending and climbing the arroyos despite its saucer shaped wheels, forcing us to use ropes to keep it from overturning. For the life of me, I couldn't figure out why they had chosen such a large wagon instead of one of the smaller Conestogas or ranch wagons.

Reluctantly, I called a halt. "Cold camp," I told them. "You boys feed and water the horses." I didn't give any instructions to the girls. I figured Elena would take care of that.

She did. By the time we had taken care of the animals, blankets had been spread and a spiderful of corn

dodgers sat on the tailgate next to a bucket of cool water drawn from the river.

We were all exhausted, but to give the boys credit, they volunteered to stand guard. Behind them, Elena gave me a smug grin. I replied, "Okay, boys. I'll stand first. Then I'll wake you. Okay?"

The relief on their faces was obvious. I figured I could keep watch a few hours, then turn it over to Bob, but George and Bernie were too young. If nothing else, I could nap in the wagon tomorrow, but any way I cut it, sleep would be mighty scarce until we reached Fort Lancaster.

George Taylor remained behind, his thin face intent. "You won't get much sleep, will you, Mr. Adams?"

"Reckon not, son." I nodded to the blankets. "You best get some rest now. Long day tomorrow." The frail boy just stared up at me, his hands behind his back. "You hear me, George. Hop to bed now."

"I got an idea, Mr. Adams. One that oughta help you get some sleep tonight." Before I could reply, George continued, his voice rising with excitement. "I could set some traps an—"

Trying to remain patient, I shook my head. The last thing I needed now was a meddling kid. "Thanks for the idea, George, but I'll take care of everything. You just go on to bed, now."

"But Mr. Adams, I—"

My temper snapped. "No! You hear me? I said *no*!"

Every head jerked around, every eye fixed on me. George's bottom lip quivered. Elena glared at me. I grimaced inwardly, well aware I had been unjust. "Look, boy. I'm sorry I yelled at you. I appreciate what you're trying to do, but the best thing for everyone right now is sleep."

The children and Elena turned back to the blankets without a word, but the chill in their silence spoke for them.

His frail shoulders slumped, George stumbled back to his bedroll beside his brother.

I felt guiltier than a farm boy sneaking a peek at a Monkey Wards catalog. The boy only wanted to help, but he could be more help by staying out of my hair. Slamming a live cartridge into the chamber on my Winchester, I climbed the side of the arroyo and squatted in the shadows of a patch of prickly pear cactus on the rim.

Overhead, the waning moon illumined the desert with a cool glow. The only sounds were an occasional moan or sigh from the children, counterpointed by the muttering nickers of the horses.

No sooner had I settled in by the cactus than I started nodding. I was in for a long night.

The Big Dipper crept around the North Star, slower than a snail up a greased bottle. Sometime during the early morning, I dozed. When I jerked awake, false dawn had lit the eastern sky.

I jumped to my feet and rushed down the slope. Suddenly, my feet got tangled, and I flipped head over heels to the clamoring tune of rattling pots and pans and yapping racket of Dog. Stars exploded in my head when I slammed into the ground.

Struggling to sit up, I focussed my eyes to see Bob staring down at me with the Sharps cocked. Behind him stood the other children, clubs and pans raised over their heads. Dog stood staring at me, his tail wagging.

George Taylor came scampering from under the wagon, jumping and shouting. "It worked! It worked! It worked!"

Elena hurried to me and helped me to my feet. She struggled to suppress her laughter. "Are you all right?"

I shook my head and looked around. Encircling the camp was a length of twine strung ankle high and fastened to a collection of pots and pans dangling under the wagon.

George rushed up to me, his thin face glowing with excitement. "See, Mr. Adams. I told you it would work."

The children, still in their bedclothes, stood gathered in a circle, hands cupped over their lips, but their eyes sparkled with laughter. They waited expectantly for my reply.

I clenched my teeth, momentarily angry, not because I tripped over the string, but because I was the butt of the children's laughter. I looked down at George. A broad grin split his upturned face, reflecting his delight at the success of his trap.

"It did do good, didn't it, Mr. Adams? Huh?"

I shrugged. A wry grin twisted my lips. "Yeah, George. It was a good trap."

All the children broke into laughter, and I laughed along with them. After all, it was a good trap.

Chapter Three

Iwas so tuckered out, I kept falling asleep in the saddle throughout the day. Mid-afternoon, I rode in, planning on a short nap. Bob climbed into the saddle to spell me. "Don't wander too far out," I cautioned him. "You see anything, hightail it back in here."

Bob pulled his hat down on his head and nodded.

"Did you hear me?"

His brows knit. "Yeah. Don't go worrying about me. I know what to do." Elena walked up behind me, and Bob puffed up his chest. "I can do it as good as you," he added, the tone in his voice daring me to disagree.

I was too sleepy to argue. "Okay."

He turned the mustang and kicked it in the flanks.

31

Elena called after him. "Be careful."

While she watched after him, I crawled into the wagon and lay down. I was asleep before she ever climbed up on the seat.

A couple hours later, rough hands shook me awake. I sat up and rubbed my eyes. My sweat-soaked clothes clung to me. "What is it?"

Elena pointed in the distance. "Bob. He's seen something. He's coming back hell-bent for leather."

She was right. Bob Chapman was bent low over the mustang's neck as the racing animal weaved through the cedar and mesquite. I looked past him, but all I could see beyond the clouds of dust raised by the mustang's hooves was a small mesa a few miles distant.

As he drew closer, he stood in the saddle and waved wildly. "Injuns! Injuns!"

The mustang slid to a stiff-legged halt. Bob jerked around in the saddle and pointed to the mesa. "Back there. Injuns. A bunch of them."

I yanked on my hat. "Get in here, Bob. Look after the children." Without giving him a chance to argue, I turned to Elena. "Lay the whip to the horses. We've got to find us some place to fort up."

Bob jumped from the saddle onto the tailgate, and I slipped into the saddle. "How far?"

The young man, his face pale, but his eyes dancing with excitement, pointed to the mesa. "A few miles beyond the mesa. They were just lazing along."

Driving my heels into the mustang's flanks, I raced ahead, waving Elena after me. I angled away from the Pecos, hoping to strike a secure sanctuary where we could stand off an Indian attack if necessary.

A mile farther, we ran across a deep arroyo with several switchbacks, each almost a quarter-of-a-mile in length. I glanced over my shoulder toward the mesa, expecting to see a line of mounted Indians, but all I saw was cedar, mesquite, and prickly-pear.

We crossed the arroyo, leaving deep, clear tracks in the sand. I nodded to Bob. ''Smooth the tracks then catch up with us. We're heading north until we can find a way down into the arroyo to hide.''

I turned back as Bob dropped off the wagon.

A mile farther, I found what I had been looking for, a cave-in on one side of the arroyo. Without hesitation, we drove into the gully and pulled up on the inside of a switchback.

Clambering up on the rim, I tugged my hat over my eyes and stared at the mesa. A thin wisp of dust rose from among the mesquite. There they were. Suddenly, back to the left, some three or four miles distant, another billow of dust rose.

Instantly, the dust near the mesa thickened, and quickly rolled across the prairie. The Indians were after someone or some thing. Slowly, the thick ribbon seemed to be angling back toward the arroyo. Anxiously, I watched.

A distant voice cut through the silence of the still air. I jerked my head around. Bob Chapman was racing toward me, waving his hands. I frowned. Now what?

He slid to a halt and pointed down the arroyo. His breath came in ragged gasps, and several seconds passed before he could finally speak. "It's Bernie. Dog chased a coyote down the gully, and he ran after him."

"Bernie? What's he doing out there?"

Bob swallowed hard. "He . . . He helped me wipe out the wagon tracks."

"Bernie? I told you to go."

The young boy dropped his gaze to the ground. "Bernie wanted to go. I didn't figure it'd hurt none."

I muttered a curse, wanting to strangle the young man. "Stay here and stay out of sight. I'll get him." I grabbed my Winchester, hoping the red-headed youngster had sense enough to hide if the Indians drew too close.

Racing along the rim of the arroyo, I heard the dog yapping. I paused and knelt beside a mesquite. Fifty yards down the gully, I spotted Bernie in a swooping bend of the arroyo, peering over the rim at something out on the prairie.

Following the direction of his gaze, I spotted his black dog barking at a patch of prickly pear. Looking closer, I saw the gray patch of a coyote backed into the cactus. Beyond them, weaving through the mesquite, rode two Indians at a gallop, drawn to the barking.

I dropped to my belly and slid the Winchester forward, my anger with Bob forgotten. Bernie yanked his head down and hid beneath the undercut bank of the arroyo.

The black dog spun as the Indians burst out of the mesquite. He jumped back and barked. Behind him, the coyote darted around the prickly pear and vanished into the surrounding mesquite.

The Indian ponies swerved around Dog and skidded to a halt. The Indians were Comanche, easily recognizable by the tinkling bells on their saddles, a brazen signature of the Comanche chief, Quanah Parker. Dog's barking became frenzied as he charged back and forth at the two jittering ponies.

One of the Comanches threw his saddle gun to his shoulder and fired at the excited animal. At the last minute, his pony spooked. The slug grazed the dog, turning its angry barking into injured yelps. The wounded creature spun, biting at the pain in his back leg. In the next instant, the second Comanche fired, knocking the dog to the ground.

I glanced at Bernie, who was peering over the rim of the arroyo. For a terrifying moment, I thought he was going to leap on the rim and race to the aid of his pet, but no sooner had the second Comanche fired than

Bernie ducked back under the rim and covered his head with his arms.

Dog lay motionless.

One of the Comanches gestured and looked around, searching for an explanation for the appearance of the black dog out in the middle of the prairie. One pointed his rifle toward the arroyo. They rode to the rim, pulling up just above Bernie.

I knew they could not spot me, but still, I moved very slowly as I set the front bead on the Comanche nearest Bernie. I cocked the hammer and took up the slack in the trigger, all the while praying the boy would not move.

Long seconds passed as they studied the sandy bed of the arroyo. Finally, they turned and rode north, toward the wagon. I took a deep breath and tightened my finger.

One brave pulled up and pointed to the bed. They had spotted the dog tracks in the sand. I hoped Bernie's weren't out there also.

Sweat rolled off my forehead and stung my eyes.

Finally, they turned and headed back onto the prairie, angling toward the cloud of dust moving in the direction of the river. With a sigh, I lowered the hammer and when they disappeared, signalled to Bernie, who hurried to my side, tears rolling down his cheeks.

"Let's go," I said, turning toward the wagon.

Bernie hesitated and looked back at Dog. "No. Dog. He's hurt. I got to help him."

I threw a rope on my impatience. I studied the boy, then glanced across the prairie. His eyes pleaded with me. I shrugged. "Okay, but we've got to stay low. Understand?"

Bernie nodded, and we ghosted across the arroyo to Dog. I knew the animal was dead, but I also knew that until Bernie saw for himself, he'd never be able to get on with his own life.

The little red-headed boy knelt by his dog and stroked the animal's head and ears for several moments. "I sure would like to bury him, but if the Comanche came back, and he was gone, they'd come looking for us." He paused, then added, "I wouldn't want to do that to the others." Somewhere in those few moments, Bernie grew up quite a bit. He looked up at me, his eyes filled with tears.

Well, that small piece of mature observation made me feel real good about Bernie. To survive the west, a jasper had to be honest with himself and do what was right. And as long as Bernie kept that kind of sensible outlook, he'd get along just fine. "Reckon you're right, boy. Now, we'd best get back to the others."

Together, we hurried back to the wagon. Now that Bernie was safe, my anger with Bob Chapman returned.

When we reached the wagon, I confronted the young man, sticking my nose right in his face. "Why didn't you do what I told you? That boy almost got killed back there. You think I talk just to hear myself talk? Well, I don't, and from now on, mister, you best listen to me." His face paled, and the usual smug curl on his lips crumbled.

Elena interrupted. "Don't you dare lay a hand on that child, Mr. Adams."

Without taking my eyes off the frightened boy, I responded to her demand, my words short and harsh. "This *child* is a stubborn, hard-headed young man who not only got Dog killed, but almost got Bernie scalped by two Comanche."

"I . . . I . . ." His voice broke and tears flooded his eyes.

I set my jaw and glared at him. "You're at the age where you got to be a man. That means you got to think growed up thoughts, not those of a child. You understand?"

All he could do was nod, but he did a good job of that.

If he'd been a man full growed, I'd probably have busted his nose across his face, but he was just a kid. "Now, get in the wagon."

I turned to Elena. "Comanche out there. From the dust, it appears to be a right sizeable force."

"What are we going to do?" Her face was tight with fear.

"Nothing. Not right now. We just stay put. Give them a chance to move on out of the country. We get out there now and kick up a cloud of dust, they'll come see what caused it." I turned to Hey and pulled off the saddle and blanket. "No. We'll just sit tight and wait for tonight."

After I rubbed Hey down, I climbed up on the arroyo rim and sat in a clump of mesquite, my eyes fixed on the slowly moving cloud of dust. I had a sinking feeling in the pit of my stomach about the destination of the Comanche. I sure hoped I was wrong.

The sky turned a brilliant shade of gold as the sun paused before dropping below the horizon. I came back into camp from where I had been watching the prairie. "Load up. Time to go."

The children glanced at each other. Elena spoke for all of them. "At night?"

"It won't be easy, but there's enough of a moon so we can see where we're going." I gestured in the direction of the Comanche. "We need to put some distance between them and us."

Rachel Sheridan stared at me, her bottom lip quivering. "Can't we just hide here. I'm afraid. Let's just stay here until the Indians are gone." Her goose stood by her side, its neck arched and its eyes fixed on me.

I forced a grin. "I wish we could, honey, but we've

got to go on. We'll be in danger if we stay or go. This way, we'll be going to someone who can help us.'' I don't know if she understood me or not, but she nodded and climbed into the wagon.

A few minutes later, we moved out, the rattle and clacking of the wagon sounding like thunder in the still of the prairie night. Occasionally, we ran into sandier soil and the rattling subsided, but there always remained the creak of the leather and grunt of the horses and the clinking of chains.

I had warned Elena to keep a tight rein on the horses, especially the leaders. Rattlesnakes moved around in the cool of the night, and odds were, we'd run across one or two. When that happened, she needed a firm hand. ''Watch me. I'll ride out front. If my animal spooks, pull up.''

She nodded, her face somber, her jaw set.

The night was long, and we were all mighty happy to see the sun peek over the eastern horizon. We pulled up about an hour after sunrise when we found a shaded nook at the base of a rocky mesa. A tiny stream of sweet water bubbled from a fissure into a small pond. Post oak shaded the pond. A hundred yards down stream, the waters disappeared into the soil.

George dug out his ball of twine and went about setting up his trip line around the camp. I didn't argue this time.

Throughout the morning, I sat under a cedar on the

mesa searching the countryside for any sign of the Comanche. Once or twice, I spotted dust far to the southwest, somewhere in the vicinity of Fort Lancaster. Comanche? Or federal troops?

I glanced to the southeast and San Antone. Only two days left before Lorenzo Scott gave up on me and pulled out of San Antone. Only two days between me and enough money to make Natalia Ludden's pa admit I wasn't a failure.

Another cloud of dust drifted up over the horizon. I clambered down the side of the mesa and saddled Hey. After giving instructions, I rode out, determined to learn the source of the dust.

If I found troops, I could point them to the mesa and get on about my own problems, namely reaching my old compadre in San Antone before he pulled out. For a moment I dreamed, thinking of Natalia and my ranch over near Bastrop, but Hey's sudden jump yanked me back to the present.

The horse squealed and skittered aside, almost throwing me from the saddle. "What the. . . . "

The buzzing hum of rattles cut through the silence. Ten feet away, a rattlesnake thick as my arm lay coiled at the base of a rotting mesquite. I shook my head and patted Hey's neck. "Easy, boy. He's just warning us." I backed Hey up a few steps and dismounted to inspect his legs. They were sound, no evidence of snakebite.

Climbing back into the saddle, I turned him toward

the dust. "Let's go, boy. Give our snake friend all the room he wants."

Two hours later, I had my answer. Two hundred Comanches, Kiowas, and Cheyenne were heading straight for Fort Lancaster.

I grimaced, shaking my head at the futility of my own situation. Every step they took toward Fort Lancaster was another shovelful of dirt on the grave of my dreams and aspirations.

Leaving Elena and the children was not even a consideration, but it was hard to sit there in the shade of mesquite and red cedar and watch my hopes disappear in a cloud of dust.

Chapter Four

Elena and the children listened soberly while I explained our predicament. "The only answer is to swing wide of Fort Lancaster and head for the upper reaches of Devil's River about sixty miles from here. From there, we can follow the river down to Fort Clark near the Rio Grande and then cut due east to San Antone." I paused. The children's faces were pale, their eyes wide with apprehension. Bernie licked his lips.

Maybe I should have tried to comfort them, but I didn't know what to say. Instead, I said, "We'll rest up today and move out in the morning."

After the children had left, Elena looked up at me even though I was only an inch or so taller than her.

"What about San Antonio? You stay with us, and you'll miss the cattle drive."

I forced an unfelt grin. "There's always another cattle drive." I tried to sound confident, but that's not how I felt.

That afternoon, I sat on the wagon tongue watching the children splashing in the pool of mountain water.

"Mind if I join you?"

Elena stood behind me. I gestured to the wagon tongue. "Help yourself."

"Strange, isn't it?" she said, sitting beside me. "Here we are out in the middle of the Texas wilderness. The children are swimming and having a good time just like they didn't have anything to worry about."

I nodded and looked at the children. They were all in the water, all except Mary Chapman who was leaning against a post oak writing in that little book of hers. I gestured to the girl. "She don't talk much, huh?"

"She used to. But when she saw her ma and pa laying on the ground all butchered, seemed like she just pulled back inside herself." She hesitated, touching her finger to her lips as she considered her words. "Back at the ranch, she always kept her diary, believing that someday, a handsome prince will come along and whisk her away to a castle in a faraway land."

I chuckled. "Not a bad dream."

Elena smiled sadly. "No, not a bad dream, but since

that day, she's never said a word . . . just writes in her diary.'' She raised her eyebrows. ''Maybe she's trying to get rid of the terror of that day.''

Mary scribbled away, oblivious to the world. I took a good look at her, at the big brown eyes that had seen more horror than any grown man should—let alone an eleven-year-old girl—at the slumped shoulders beneath a worn dress of calico blue, at the dusty and runover hightop shoes.

My shoulders sagged in helpless frustration. ''Well, let her scribble if it helps.''

A sudden peal of laughter jerked my eyes back to the children in the pond. A full-fledged, give-no-quarter water fight was taking place. I started to yell at them to quiet down, but I held my words. Let them enjoy themselves today. They were going to need every ounce of that spirit for the overland trip to Devil's River.

I awakened Bob for the three o'clock shift. ''Just squat by these cedars, and keep your eyes open. I don't expect you'll spot anything, but keep an eye peeled anyway.''

He grunted and tugged his battered hat down on his head. ''You don't have to tell me what to do. I know how to keep a lookout.''

I bit my tongue and pointed to the trees. ''Then do it.''

Without waiting for a reply from the sullen boy, I

rolled out my bedroll and climbed between the blankets. I laced my fingers together behind my head and stared at the dazzling display of stars above, wide awake, remembering my own youth.

Had I spoken to my pa like Bob spoke to me, I'd have been picking myself up off the ground. We were taught to respect our elders, not like these youngsters today.

It seemed as if these kids felt a jasper had to earn courtesy and respect a dozen times a day. Earn. That's what bothered me. I had always figured that courtesy was the easiest way to get along with everyone and respect was something you naturally paid a person who had weathered the hard struggles of this life a little longer than you had.

I sighed. Who knows? Life was changing fast, and a whole, brand-spanking-new generation was chomping at the bit. As far as I was concerned, I'd gladly let them take over and straighten out the world. All I wanted to do was get this herd of youngsters to San Antone and get on with my life.

Pulling the blanket about my neck, I rolled over. Philosophizing always made me sleepy.

I rolled out of my blankets just before sunrise, still tired. Three hours of sleep didn't perk me up too much, but it was better than nothing.

Bob had a small fire going. He glared at me defensively when I approached the fire and held out my hands to warm them. I glanced at him, nodded, and remained silent.

The set to his jaw softened, and he nodded to the fire. ''There's coffee,'' he said, turning back to his post in the darkness.

Squatting by the fire, I sipped some of his coffee. I was surprised to find it was good, better than my own if the truth be told. I cut my eyes toward the boy, understanding exactly why he had gone to all the trouble of building the fire and boiling the coffee. Yep, he was growing up. Too bad it was so painful, but that's the price a jasper paid to be a man.

I shook my head and pushed all those deep thoughts aside. I didn't want to give myself a headache so early in the morning.

''Good morning.''

I looked around as Elena approached. Behind her, the children began stumbling from their blankets, and the morning routine lurched into action with Bernie taking the lead.

An hour later, we were ready to pull out.

Something tugged at my shirt sleeve. ''We can't go yet,'' whispered Rachel Sheridan, staring up at me.

I glanced at Elena who shook her head and squatted in front of the girl. ''Why not, honey?'' she asked.

She pointed to the mesa looming above us. '' 'Cause Mary ain't back yet.''

Elena looked around the camp, quickly counting

heads. She cut her eyes to me. "Have you seen Mary this morning?"

I spun on Bob. "Did you let her leave camp, boy?"

His eyes narrowed. "No. I didn't. And my name ain't boy. It's Bob."

My cheeks burned with anger. Before I could reply, Rachel spoke up. "Mary left last night, Mr. Adams. Before we went to bed."

Elena spoke gently. "Where is she, Rachel?"

She pointed to the mesa again. "Up there. Writing in her book. She said up there would put her closer to her dreams."

I rolled my eyes. At that moment, I was absolutely positive we would never, never, never reach San Antone. In fact, looking back over the past few days, I'd had more trouble from these kids than the Comanche.

"Well, I reckon I'd better go get that girl of yours," I said, directing my frustration at Elena.

Her brows knitted in anger, then her eyes focussed on something behind me and her face softened into a smile. "You won't have to, Mr. Adams. Here she comes now."

Mary Chapman strolled into camp, her folded arms holding her diary to her chest. She halted when she realized everyone was staring at her.

I took a step toward her, but Elena laid her hand on my arm.

Bob spoke up. "You better get back in here, you dumb girl. I—"

Elena stopped him. "Hush, Bob. Don't talk to your sister like that."

"But—"

"I said hush."

He dropped his eyes, and Mary, like a little queen, tilted her jaw, marched across the camp, climbed into the wagon, and took her seat.

I looked around at Elena. She stared up at me, her face solemn. "I told you about her."

Before we pulled out, I climbed the mesa and searched the countryside, studying our route. I shook my head. We were not in for an easy time. To the northwest, two antelope bounced across the prairie. I watched the graceful animals as they disappeared into some post oaks brakes far behind us.

Suddenly, a flash of light cut through the early morning shadows and just as quickly, disappeared. I dropped to one knee and studied the far shadows, searching for some movement. I strained to hear any unusual sounds. Nothing. Finally, I clambered down the steep trail, pushing the flash of light into the back of my mind, but not forgetting about it.

Travelling grew more difficult as the terrain grew rougher. I cursed that awkward, lumbering wagon, once or twice considering chopping it in half. After all, there was an axe in the tool box.

The second night from the mesa, I asked Elena about it.

She glanced at the wagon. "What do you mean, wasn't there another wagon we could have taken?"

"Just what I said. Why did you choose this wagon instead of another?"

Her gaze darted back to the wagon before settling on me. She drew the tip of her tongue across her lips. "It . . . It was the only one left. The others had been burned by the Comanche."

I poured another cup of coffee and leaned back against a small post oak. "I just wondered."

She considered our conversation for a few seconds. "Does the country get rougher ahead?"

"Don't know. I've never been right through here, but from the looks of what we've crossed the last couple days, I'm figuring we're in for a lot harder time. I know that to the northeast and east, there's a range of rough country. Not mountains, but they'll give a man the same kind of trouble."

We pulled out at sunrise next morning, hoping to hit Devil's River by nightfall. We came up short by several miles so we hauled up at a copse of post oak deep in a rocky canyon just before sundown.

We built a small fire and quickly boiled some coffee and heated beans and cornbread. Just as quickly, we extinguished the fire and settled into our blankets.

During my night watch, I wondered again about the

flash of light I had spotted from the mesa the previous morning. I wanted to dismiss it as simply a reflection off water or maybe even an outcropping of mica, but I'd spent too much time in the wilderness to dismiss anything without being absolutely certain.

I'd seen enough Apaches materialize from the ground almost at my feet to take any chances, so to be on the safe side, I had kept watch on our backtrail throughout the day's journey.

The night passed without event. Once or twice, I heard some faint noises to the south, but figured it was foraging deer or coyotes. After breakfast, we pulled out of the canyon and set our course for Devil's River.

The morning was crisp and clear, the air sweet, the sky blue. Overhead, a red-tailed hawk glided on the currents, and in the treetops, larks sang a lilting melody. I drew a deep breath.

A rider burst out of a patch of cedar, his hand filled with a sixgun. "Hold it, folks. You're covered."

Chapter Five

In the next instant, a sharp click sounded from behind. I jerked around to see a second outlaw holding a Winchester centered on my chest. He leered at me. "Well, well, well. Howdy, Buster. Imagine running across you out here. Reckon luck's done smiled on me."

My blood ran cold. Cheyenne Bill Longstrum. One of the bloodiest butchers to haunt the *despoblado*.

His gray hair hung in greasy ropes over the shoulders of his dirt-crusted buckskins and his big grin revealed a mouthful of rotted teeth. He still wore the same tattered eagle feather in his hat. He waved the muzzle of his Winchester in a small circle. "Looks like I'm going to get me two birds with the one shot, don't it,

Two Bit?'' he yelled at his partner. ''Makes all them miles from the border worthwhile, don't it, Two Bit?''

His compadre rode up to the lead horses. ''It shore do, Bill. It shore do.'' His eyes locked on Elena. He licked his lips. ''One is right purty, too.''

My mind raced, searching for a way out. I'd run across Cheyenne Bill on occasion, even worked on the same freight line, but never had no truck with him. While I despised him as a human being, I respected his skill with a sixgun.

One of the children stood up in the wagon. Instantly, Bill and Two Bit's guns leaped around. I yelled. ''You kids sit. Don't move.''

''An' keep your yaps shut,'' barked Bill.

The children remained silent, but Sally, the goose, picked this time to display her independence. Flapping her wings, she rose on her webbed feet and hissed.

''You better hold on to that duck, kid, or me and Two Bit is gonna have us a prime supper tonight,'' yelled Bill.

Rachel threw her arms around the goose, but Sally was not to be deterred. She squawked and squirmed her neck from Rachel's arms and shot into the air, flapping her wings as she made straight for Cheyenne Bill. The goose slammed into his horse's head, causing the animal to rear and paw the air.

Bill dropped the Winchester and grabbed the saddle horn.

I leaped from my saddle, shucking my sixgun in mid-air. I hit the ground and rolled, snapping off three fast slugs. All three caught Two Bit in the chest, knocking him from the saddle.

Rolling onto my back, I tried to draw a bead on Bill, but between the sunfishing of his frightened pony and the buffeting wings of Sally the goose, it was like hitting a housefly that had been sipping at homemade corn whiskey.

Spurring his horse, Bill drove the animal into the stand of post oak from which he had appeared, ducking under a low-hanging limb. The limb caught Sally, and with a loud squawk, she tumbled to the ground, wings flapping. Instantly, she jumped to her feet, hissing, her neck arched, her wings flapping.

I snapped off a shot at Bill just as he disappeared in the depths of the post oak brake. I missed, but from the fading beat of his galloping horse, he was trying to put some distance between us. For a moment, I considered pursuing, but I didn't want to take a chance on leaving Elena and the children by themselves.

"Anyone hurt?" I asked, reloading my sixgun.

"No. We . . . We're all fine," said Elena, her voice subdued.

We had no shovel, so I pulled the dead outlaw near the rocky wall of a narrow canyon and covered him with boulders after removing his gunbelt. I tossed the belt under the seat of the freight wagon and tied his horse to the tailgate.

George Taylor spoke up. "You sure are fast, Mr. Adams. Are you a gunfighter?"

I looked at him in surprise. All of the children except Bob Chapman were staring at me, like this was the first time they had really seen me. I wouldn't call it admiration or respect, but rather awe. Growing up on a ranch the way most of them had, chances were they'd never seen a gunfight, not that it was pleasant to behold, but in the cowtowns of the west, such confrontations were commonplace.

"No," I replied, grinning to myself. "I'm no gunfighter, George."

"Yeah," chimed in Bernie. "But you're fast. You oughta be one."

Elena's face grew stern. I spoke before she had a chance. "A gunfighter's life is a dead-end, Bernie. Only one thing a gunman can depend on."

"What's that? His gun?"

Bernie leaned forward expectantly. I shook my head and nodded to the pile of rocks on the side of the canyon. "No. A grave. That's the only thing a gunfighter can depend on, a grave, like that one."

"But . . ."

Bob Chapman interrupted George. "Yeah? So what? We all die."

The young man stood glaring at me, his Sharps cradled in the crook of his arm. His jaw was set, but he couldn't still the tiny quiver in his lips. I didn't want to argue with him, and sure as I was breathing, that's exactly what he was trying to dredge up.

"I can't argue with you about that, Bob. We all die. The only thing is that a man ought to live more than twenty years. Me, I'm seven or eight years past that point, and I'd sure like to see another thirty or forty before I cash in."

I looked into Bob Chapman's eyes, but I could tell he didn't believe a word I said. I shook my head. "Let's get a move on. We want to reach the river before sunset."

Elena hesitated, her eyes fixed on mine, her cool demeanor asking the question that Cheyenne Bill had raised. I explained. "I ran across Bill when I was bullwhacking for the El Paso Freight line. He worked for the line until he was fired for stealing goods and selling them at a discount to merchants. A few weeks after he was fired, him and a couple of his sidewinders tried to hold us up just outside of El Paso. We killed one of his men, but him and the other escaped." I nodded to the grave in the canyon. "That was probably the same jasper."

She studied me a moment, then a smile played over her lips. Tugging her flat-brimmed hat over her eyes, she climbed back onto the wagon seat and reached for the reins.

The remainder of the day was uneventful, giving me time to replay the confrontation with the two outlaws. Slowly, as I studied over the morning, a few randon events of the last few days took on a different perspective. Cheyenne Bill Longstrum's remark, *makes all them miles from the border worthwhile* stirred up a whole panful of questions in my brain.

Had he followed the wagon all the way from the border? Why? If he had, he could have been the source of the few wisps of dust I had attributed to dust devils, perhaps even the cloud of dust chased by the Comanche.

I glanced at the large wagon bouncing and rattling across the prairie, at the young woman handling the reins like she was born to them. What was so valuable about her or the children for Bill and his sidekick to track them over two hundred miles?

Could Elena and the children be witnesses to the actual murder of their families? They claimed Comanches killed their folks. Nothing had been said about white renegades.

We reached Devil's River in mid-afternoon, and I hadn't made sense out of anything that had happened. All I knew was that in a couple days, we'd reach Fort Clark. Then we'd be safe.

We set up camp in a secluded canyon. After a spare

meal, we made ready for bed. George set up his traps once again, now a nightly routine. I took my bedroll and climbed to the top of the canyon. The country lay beneath me for miles, and Devil's River twisted and turned through the dark forest like a silver snake in the night.

Suddenly, a light flickered to the southwest, then vanished. I rubbed my eyes. Had I imagined the light? No. I had imagined nothing. I saw a light, but whose? Comanche? I didn't think so. Had it been the Comanche, there would have been several fires. A single fire suggested a small group, no more than four or five.

Then I knew. I closed my eyes and leaned back against a boulder and muttered a curse. Cheyenne Bill Longstrum.

Moving silently, I slipped into our camp and awakened Bob and Elena. I told them of the fire. "Both of you keep watch. Bob, you take your Sharps and find a spot west of the camp." I handed Elena the outlaw's sixgun. "There's a small patch of cedar south of the camp. Hide in there."

Bob nodded, his eyes wide with excitement. Elena whispered, "What about you?"

"I've got to find out who's down there. It might be nothing for us to worry about."

The waning moon was only a thin crescent, and thick shadows covered the prairie like black smoke. While

I had only spotted a glimmer of the fire for an instant, I guessed it was a couple miles downriver.

I stayed in the shadows, circling clear areas when I came to them. Suddenly, I smelled woodsmoke. I dropped to my knees and stared into the darkness. Nothing. After a moment, I rose to a crouch and slipped in the direction of the smoke.

Minutes later, I spotted the flames of a small fire. Pausing to study the area around me, I eased to my right, not wanting to be trapped against the bank of the river. I fell to my belly and glided beneath the undergrowth to within a short distance of the fire.

Four men squatted around the fire, sipping on coffee. I doubled my fist when I recognized Cheyenne Bill Longstrum. I studied the other three, wondering just where they had come from. Still too far to make out their conversation, I squirmed forward on my stomach, moving only when one of them spoke.

"I say, let's surprise 'em in the morning. There's four of us." The outlaw rose and scratched his thick belly.

Bill shook his head. "Half-a-day's ride from here, the river cuts through a narrow canyon. There's room on one bank for the wagon. Perfect spot for us to jump 'em."

Thick belly grunted. "This jasper be as smart as you say, they might go around."

"No." Bill drained his coffee. "It'll be a three day delay to go around. They'll go through."

The first outlaw sneered. "I still say, we oughta just jump 'em."

Cheyenne Bill rapped his empty cup on his knee to dispell the last few drops of coffee. "Buster Adams might be a small man, and he might not be a gunfighter, but he shoots straighter and fights longer than any man I ever knowed. I got me a choice of ambushing him or meeting him head on, I'll take ambush ever' time."

The first outlaw eyed Bill for a moment, then shrugged. "Whatever you say."

Back at the camp, I told Elena and the children what I had learned.

"What are we going to do?" she asked.

Bob spoke up. "We got guns. Let's shoot our way through."

Bernie groaned. "That's just about the dumbest thing I ever heard. Why—"

Bob spun on him. "You shut up, you—"

I didn't wait for Elena to stop them this time. "Both of you shut up!" My words slapped their faces. As one, they jerked around to look at me. "I mean it. We don't have time for squabbles. Now you two both keep your mouths closed. You hear?"

Bernie nodded quickly, but Bob just glared at me. I turned back to Elena. "There's four of them. We might get one or two, but that's all. Our best bet is that way." I pointed to the river. "San Antone is about two hundred miles to the southeast. We cross and set up an ambush. If it works, we can cut south toward Fort Clark."

Elena looked at the swift river. "Do you think we can get the wagon across? It's heavy."

"Maybe, but it's wood. We can make it. We'll wrap the canvas around the bed to keep most of the water out. Bob and I will take the horses across and use them to drag the wagon over with the children inside."

"Yes, but the axles are hickory. And the tires are steel. What if it sinks?"

"It won't. We'll get it across."

"Are you sure?"

For some reason, she seemed particularly concerned about the wagon. Naturally, we needed it for transportation, but there appeared to be something more involved. I pushed it from my mind. I had enough to worry about. "I'm telling you, it won't sink."

She parted her lips to speak, hesitated, then said, "If you say so."

The girls' eyes grew wide. Rachel looked up at Elena. "I'm scared."

Elena spoke gently, "I'll be with you, Rachel. We'll be just fine."

From the look on her face, I knew she was just as scared as the child, but she was sure showing some grit.

While the boys wrapped the wagon, I cast up and down the river, looking for an ideal crossing. A few hundred feet above us, I discovered a shallow, rock-bottomed ford, both banks of which were also solid rock.

By rigging lines front and back, we would float the wagon across the churning river. After instructing Bob, still sullen, how to harness the ropes to the doubletree, I led the team across while the young boy played out the rope behind. Once I reached the far shore, he snugged down the ropes to the O-rings on the doubletree, and I tied the lead horses to a post oak.

Then we swapped sides of the river. Bob untied the team while I lashed one end of a stout rope around the rear bolster of the wagon and with the other, took a single loop around the trunk of an oak. Now, we had the wagon lashed front and back.

When I was ready, I signaled the young boy. He waved back. "Ready?" I shouted to Elena who sat in the bed with the children around her.

She whispered to the kids, and they all nodded. "Ready."

I waved to Bob, and he started the horses. I played out the rope, keeping it taut as the lumbering freight wagon rolled into the river.

The force of the river struck the wagon broadside, forcing it down river. The ropes hummed with strain. Across the river, the team lowered their heads, throwing their shoulders into the sudden struggle placed upon them.

I kept waiting for the wagon to float as the water crept nearer the top of the sideboards, but the heavy wheels bounced and jerked over the river bed. Finally, when the water was less than six inches from flooding, the wagon broke free of the rocky bottom, bobbed once, and whipped downstream in the swift current.

The sudden jerk ripped the rope from my hands, burning my palms. Before I could grab the loose end, the rope zipped around the tree and snaked across the river bank toward the water.

I leaped for the rope. Grabbing the end, I raced to a smaller oak near the river. The current was quickly taking up the slack. I whipped the end of the rope around the trunk and held on with all my strength as the rope popped taut.

The wagon wallowed in the current, water splashing over the sideboards. The children screamed. Elena, her face whiter than the blouse she wore, tried to calm them.

Across the river, the sudden strain staggered the horses, and yanked them back toward the river.

"Drive 'em out of there," I yelled, but the roar of the river drowned my words.

Bob Chapman handled the team like an old hand, gently urging the straining animals forward. For long seconds, the power of the river defied the groaning horses. Their hooves skidded on the rocky plate, and step by step, they were pulled closer and closer to the water.

The young man remained cool, still quietly prodding the animals. Their backward progress slowed, then finally, the team matched the strength of the current. Bob picked up his entreaties, goading the straining beasts forward.

Step by small step, they began dragging the wagon across the river. Finally, the wagon rolled ashore.

I climbed into the saddle and led the outlaw's horse across. Within minutes, we had hitched the team to the wagon and moved out, planning on swinging south before cutting back to Fort Clark.

Bob rode drag on the outlaw's horse while I rode point. With luck, we just might slip by Longstrum and his men. I figured it would be morning before they decided we weren't following the river. But, there was no question in my mind that they would find us. Our tracks were impossible to hide.

All we were doing was buying time, forcing them to come to us on our terms, on our ground. Within the next few hours, we had to decide our course of action when they found us. Running was no answer.

In the middle of the afternoon, the good Lord smiled on us. A heavy wind blew in from the east, pushing thick clouds across the hills and canyons. Soon the storm swept in from out of the southeast, one of those powerful storms that come raging out of the Gulf of Mexico this time of the year.

Elena grinned at me when the rain struck, her teeth a brilliant white against her sun-darkened skin. "Just what we need."

I didn't want to alarm her, so I nodded agreement.

If the storm was like others, we were in for several hours of weather. We needed to find a place to hole up. I motioned the wagon into a patch of post oak at the base of a cliff. "I'll scout around. See what I can find."

Bob sat on his horse, soaked to the skin like me. "I'll go with you."

I wiped the rain from my face. "I need you here, Bob. To look after the kids."

A mixture of stubbornness and pride filled his face. He straightened his shoulders and looked me square in the eye. "Okay."

I guessed that these rocky canyons were filled with caves. The right one would provide security and shelter. I didn't want to upset Elena or the children, but I figured this weather wouldn't stop Cheyenne Bill and his men.

At first appearance, the canyon seemed shallow, but behind a copse of cedar, I discovered a narrow trail, which opened into another canyon. A short distance back in the second canyon, I stumbled across a trail leading up the side of the rocky wall. Dismounting, I followed the trail to a wide fissure in the granite escarpment. Entering the fissure, I discovered a deep cave, large enough for twice our number in addition to our animals. Long dead ashes were scattered across the sandy floor.

The entrance to the cave could not be seen from outside, and only by climbing some boulders could I see the freight wagon in the post oaks below.

The storm intensified. Quickly we hauled our supplies up the trail to the cave. While Bob and I coaxed our two ponies up the rain slick slope, Bernie started a small fire at the rear of the cave. A natural draft pulled the smoke into a fracture in the ceiling.

Elena lit a candle from her supplies and fixed it to an outcropping of rock. ''You girls lay out the bedrolls over there.'' She turned to me. ''What about the wagon and horses?'' Elena asked. ''We can't leave them there.''

''No place to put them. There's not enough room in here for six more horses, and the wagon is too wide to fit through the trail into the second canyon.''

My explanation should have satisfied her, but for some reason, she seemed uneasy.

''Don't worry,'' I added. ''I'm going down and hobble the horses. They'll be there when the storm breaks.''

The storm howled at the mouth of the cave throughout the night. The morning dawned gray and dreary, the rain pelting the rocky threshold of the cave. Bob stirred the banked fire, but I stopped him. "Let me take a look outside first."

Consternation knitted his forehead. "You think someone's out there?"

I tugged my hat on tight. "Doubt it, but you never can tell. You wait here. I'll be back directly."

Throwing my slicker over my head, I stepped into the gusting rain. The direction had shifted to the southwest, indicating that the storm was passing. I climbed to the boulders above the cave and peered down upon the wagon and horses.

Instantly, I pressed my body against the boulders, sliding back in the same motion. Below, four men were sitting on their horses staring at the wagon.

Longstrum!

I cursed and hurried back to the cave to warn Elena and the children to keep quiet. Then I returned to the boulders on the point of the canyon.

Removing my hat, I eased into position so I could peer through the crack between two boulders. One of the hombres tore off the canvas top and pulled the oaken bows from their sockets. A second pulled the axe from the tool box and began chopping up the floor of the wagon. A third slashed the hobbles on the horses and reached for the harness.

The man with the axe yelled. "Here! Here it is!"

Chapter Six

When the jasper harnessing the horses heard the shout, he threw the bridle to the ground and splashed through the mud to the wagon.

One man was bent over in the bed of the wagon, straining to lift something. I tried to see what they were so excited about, but the other three blocked my vision.

Suddenly, the man lurched backward, losing his balance and falling out of the wagon. In one hand was a board from the floor of the wagon. The axe was in the other, but it flew out of his hand into some nearby undergrowth.

Before any of them could move, gunfire broke out. I looked up to see a horde of Comanches charging out of the undergrowth, rifles firing.

The draft horses scattered. Longstrum leaped on his pony and skedaddled. His men were not so fortunate. They managed to get off only a few shots before they were overwhelmed. Hurriedly, I slipped from the boulders and raced back to the cave.

Bob and Elena stood just inside the mouth of the cave, their guns cocked and ready. I told them what was happening. "Just stay in here. I'm slipping back up. Keep the kids quiet."

Elena laid her hand on my arm. "Be careful."

I paused and looked into her dark eyes. "I will."

Palming my .44, I eased back into the boulders, grateful for the stormy weather. Below, several Comanches whooped and hollered over the dead white men while others tore up the bed of the wagon.

My eyes popped open when I saw the gold bars and jewels hidden beneath the floor of the wagon. Suddenly, all of the vague and fuzzy explanations became clear. Now I knew why Elena had selected the wagon. Now I knew why the tires cut so deeply into the soil. Now I knew why the wagon could barely float the river.

My ears burned when I thought how Elena's greed had endangered all of us. I shot a withering look back at the cave. She was due a tongue-lashing she would never forget.

For the present, I remained in the boulders, keeping an eye on the Comanche. They tried to fire the wagon, but the rain extinguished the fire.

Finally, they departed, heading directly for Fort Clark. I watched until they disappeared over the horizon, and then, jaw set, I turned back to the cave, furious over the deception that had blown my dreams higher than a cartwheeling bronc.

I don't know which upset Elena more, my vehement upbraiding of her motives or the knowledge that the gold and jewels were now the property of thirty or forty Comanches. Whichever it was, tears were rolling down her cheeks when I finished, but she never once dropped her eyes, not once. They remained fixed on mine throughout the entire tirade, never wavering while I singed her hide.

I paused, then added, "Don't you realize you could have gotten all of us killed just because of the gold and jewels?"

The muscles in her jaw squirmed like a clutch of snakes. "It was worth the risk."

All I could do was stare at her.

The children, who had been standing aside, had slowly gathered behind her while I ranted and raved, and now presented an almost solid front—except for Mary. She sat with her back to the wall, writing in her diary.

"Worth the risk? Is that what you're trying to tell me?"

Tears welled in her eyes again. "Maybe I was wrong. I can't tell the future. All I knew was that I had five orphanned kids, and we needed money to take care of us when we reached San Antonio. I've seen too many children in orphanages. These children weren't going to end up like that. With the gold and jewels, we could have found us a small place near a civilized town like Austin.''

I tried to stare her down, but her reply had knocked the wind from me. Instead, I glared at the children. They glared back, and Rachel waddled over to take Elena's hand. She glared at me too.

A wise man knows when he's licked, but I wasn't going to admit it. With as much dignity as I could muster, I spun on my heel and headed for the door. ''Wait here,'' I called over my shoulder.

After studying the countryside around us, I returned to the cave for Bob. We saddled our ponies and together, we found four of the draft horses and hitched them to the wagon. I made it a point to retrieve the axe and what other tools the Comanches had slung to the ground.

No one said a word as they climbed into the wagon. A faint blush tinged Elena's cheeks as she picked up the reins, but she smartly brought the lead horses around and pointed them west.

I pulled up beside her. ''Not that way. We go southeast.''

Bob reined up as Elena protested. ''But, that's the way to Fort Clark.''

''We're not going to Fort Clark,'' I said. I started

to explain, but still angry over her lies, I deliberately refused to say more.

"Why not?"

"Yeah," chimed in Bob. "Why not?" His tone was challenging.

"Because that's the direction the Comanches headed." I couldn't resist adding to Elena, "I hope you're satisfied. If you hadn't brought the gold, Longstrum wouldn't have followed and drawn the Comanches to us. Now we've got to head across some of the roughest country in the state to reach San Antone . . . if we ever reach it."

She stared up at me, tears welling in her eyes, her lips quivering. Maybe I should have taken some satisfaction in putting her in her place, but I felt no pleasure at all, just an overwhelming emptiness inside.

The next day was a nightmare.

That morning, Mary, the quiet young girl, vomited and lay doubled over, clutching her stomach, responding to our questions with only a nod of her head, never a word. Finally she dropped into a fitful, exhausted sleep. At noon, the wagon bounced over a large rock and bent one of the steel tires, the shock of which awakened her. She began crying and holding her ear.

"What's wrong?" I asked.

Mary shook her head and cried.

"Just tell us so we can help," I said, pleading.

She shook her head and cried louder.

Elena held the girl in her arms and soothed her. I had to admire Elena's patience with the child. I knew Mary had been through a lot, but she could at least tell us what was wrong with her instead of just nodding or shaking her head and crying.

Finally Elena looked up at me. "Earache. She's got an earache."

I was no smoker, but I knew the benefits of warm smoke for an earache. Tearing off a small piece of canvas, I wrapped it around some crushed sage and cedar and lit it. The taste gagged me, but I managed to blow several mouthfuls of warm smoke in her ear.

Elena looked on with an arched eyebrow.

"It always worked on me," I told her.

After a while, Mary's crying grew weaker, whether because the ache had lessened or she had exhausted herself, I wasn't sure, but when she dropped off, I drove us forward.

Within a quarter-of-a-mile, the bent tire slowly worked its way off the rim. When we noticed it, we stopped and beat the tire back on the wheel. The clanging of hammer against steel awakened Mary, and again she started crying and vomiting.

From then on, every mile or so, we had to stop and beat the tire back onto the wheel, awakening Mary each time until toward the end of the day. By then, the young girl was too exhausted to wake up.

Bob took over driving the wagon while Elena sat in

the bed beside Mary, washing the sleeping child's face with a damp cloth. She looked at me, her eyes filled with pain. "Isn't there anything we can do for her?"

I knew a couple remedies, but they would take a while to prepare even if I could find the ingredients. I couldn't afford to take the time away from our travel. "We'll camp early. I'll take care of her."

A weak smile curled her lips, and she turned her attention back to Mary, who tossed and tumbled in a restless slumber.

An hour before we made camp, the rear wheel began squeaking with each revolution, a long shuddering groan that rose to a shrill screech, standing my hair on end.

By the time we stopped, the wheel was squalling like a stuck hog. I sent Bob to chop down a small oak while George and Bernie built a fire. Elena put on coffee and boiled some beans.

I gathered a couple handfuls of cedar twigs and needles and boiled them in water. Urging Mary to drink a little, I hoped it would relax and settle her stomach. She immediately tossed it back up. We tried once again, this time with no more success than the first.

"What do we do now?" asked Elena, noticeably distressed.

I looked down at the pale child, her eyes closed, her breathing shallow. "Give her a few minutes. Maybe she kept enough down to help."

Elena looked at me. "Are you sure it will help?"

Bob grunted. "Well, I ain't never heard of boiled cedar helping no one. If you ask me, we—"

"No one's asking you." I snapped at him. "Just be quiet." I looked at Elena. "It helped me a lot of times. I reckon it'll take care of her." I nodded to the bed beside the child. "Best you try to get some sleep now. The boys and me got work to do."

We put out the fire and lit one of Elena's candles so we could see to repair the wagon. Stacking rocks behind the wagon, we used the oak for a lever to raise the wagon so we could pull the wheel and grease the axle, using the contents of the grease bucket dangling under the wagon.

Bob, sullen and quiet, helped me slide the wheel back on the axle, and I spun the nut and tightened it down. "Now that front wheel," I muttered as we lowered the wagon.

Bob frowned. "How you goin' to fix it?" George and Bernie eased forward, curious.

I stared at the wheel. "Not sure. Best way is to heat the wheel and hammer it on; then soak it in water." I looked around the patch of oak in which we had camped. "But this isn't the time or place."

George tugged on my sleeve. I looked down at him. He grinned. "Why don't you tie it, Mr. Adams?"

I started to laugh, but then I considered his question. After all, his trip lines worked. Tie it? Why not? Lace a rope between each spoke around the entire wheel.

We were only one day to the river, and the lariat would not wear through in such a short time.

I mussed George's hair. "Good idea, boy. Let's do it." We tied one end of the lariat around the rim, then laced it between two spokes, looped it around the rim and tire, and then back through the next set of spokes. When we finished, I stepped back and studied our handiwork. It wasn't pretty, but at least we wouldn't be waking Mary every hour.

Mary? I'd forgotten about her. I peeked into the bed of the wagon, and the child was sleeping peacefully. Elena smiled at me. The medicine had worked.

I looked at Bob, but he was staring into the darkness, his jaw set.

George set up his trip line around the camp, and everyone crawled into their blankets, except me, naturally. I took my place under a small oak outside of camp.

George's idea, just as his trip line, worked well. Mary slept peacefully the next day, and we reached the river before dark, luckily stumbling onto a shallow crossing that we took before setting up camp in a secluded canyon. I wasn't exactly sure where we were. I guessed the river was either the West Nueces or the South Llano, but one fact for certain, the country was becoming more rugged.

We spent the next two days repairing the wagon.

Early morning of the second night, I sat nodding at my post when a subtle noise alerted me. Without moving a muscle, I peered into the surrounding darkness. Probably a rabbit, or maybe a prowling coyote. Any number of animals, but in the west, a man assumed nothing. If he did, he would get mighty dead mighty fast.

I strained to hear beneath the gentle sounds of the night. There it was again, a silky whisper, like two pieces of canvas rubbed together. I focussed on the bulky shadows of the nearby undergrowth from where the sound seemed to come. A leaf moved.

I remained motionless.

From the shadow, slipped a darker shadow. It was the figure of a man. A cloying odor of rancid grease stung my nostrils. Comanche!

I tightened my grip on the Winchester, searching the area for others, but I saw only one. I had an open shot at him, but the report could signal our location to the other Comanche, for rest assured, he was not out here by himself. This was a scouting party.

While I was trying to decide on my next step, George rose from his bed under the wagon and called to Bernie. "Come on, Bernie. I got to go."

Bernie's sleepy voice replied. "Go by yourself, George. I'm sleepy."

George begged.

Bernie refused.

Finally, Elena's voice came from inside the wagon. "Go with your brother, Bernie. Let the rest of us get some sleep."

The exchange kept the Comanche's attention, just long enough for me to rise into a crouch. I wanted to take care of him without gunfire.

The brave remained motionless, his head turning slightly to follow George and Bernie into the night. After a moment, the two boys returned.

My legs ached from remaining in a crouch. The Comanche did not move. Finally, ten minutes later, he started to rise.

I took a step toward him and whistled. He jerked around, and I slammed the barrel of the Winchester into his temple. He dropped like a pole-axed steer.

Immediately, I dropped into a crouch in a patch of shadows and waited. Seconds became minutes, long, tense minutes, but I heard nothing, saw nothing.

Moving quietly, I awakened the others, and we pulled out within minutes.

Mid-morning, we crossed a post oak savannah and nooned in the shade of a rocky bluff that rose from the prairie. Bob Chapman, despite his attitude, was becoming a dependable hand. I asked him to scoot up to the bluff and see what he could see. Still sullen, he did as I asked.

Ten minutes later, he came rushing back into camp. "Comanches. A few miles north, heading this-a-way. Ten or twelve. I didn't stop to get a right count."

I muttered a silent curse as I hastily surveyed the country around us. There was no place to hide.

"Up there," said Bob, understanding my dilemma and pointing to the bluff. "We can hide up there."

"What about the wagon?"

He nodded vigorously. "We can get it up there. There's some small shin oak we can pull into."

I looked at Elena, hoping she would help me decide, but from the fear in her eyes, I knew I had to decide by myself. I looked at Bob. "You're sure we can hide up there."

His face darkened. "I said we could, didn't I?"

"Then, let's get it done," I said, letting his smart remark pass.

Young Bob Chapman was right. We had to hitch Hey and the other pony to the wagon, but we reached the top and pulled into the shin oak. I yanked off the canvas top and removed the oaken bows from their sockets, lowering our profile below that of the shin oak.

Next came the time for the Great Silence. The time for us to blend in with the rugged countryside, to become part of it just as the trees and grass and rocks.

Elena and the girls lay on the blankets spread in the shade beneath the wagon. George and Bernie sat with them. Rachel whimpered, and Bernie tried to soothe her. "Everything'll be okay, Rachel. Don't worry."

The bluff on which we hid was like a finger pointing west. I put Bob on the south side of the finger, and I took the north.

Just in time. The band of Comanches rode out of a post oak brake less than half-a-mile distant.

I glanced back at the savannah and my heart thudded against my chest. The sweeping plain below was lush with tall grasses, cane bluestem, Indiangrass, little bluestem, and switchgrass—a rolling sea of grass—and slashing right through the middle of the grass were the two parallel tracks our wheels had cut in the thick growth.

The Comanche braves drew closer. Within minutes, they would cross our trail, a trail obvious even to a blind man. I hoped the path we took to the top of the bluff was the only one. We couldn't hold several approaches. I held my breath.

Suddenly, the lead pony reared and pawed the air. Exclamations erupted from the Comanche as a frightened coyote exploded from beneath his pony's feet. With wild shouts of glee at the opportunity for a brief respite from the wearisome boredom of travel, the warriors dug their heels into their ponies and sped across the savannah in pell-mell pursuit of the scampering, zig-zagging coyote.

They stormed across our trail without a second glance.

I released my breath and laid my head on my arm. We were lucky, but I reminded myself that the only sure thing about luck is that it will change. I just hoped we reached San Antone before ours turned bad.

Chapter Seven

"Were they the same Indians who came during the storm?" Elena looked up at me, her tanned face a mixture of fear and hope.

I could only shrug. "Couldn't tell."

The children were standing around us, looking on curiously. None understood the implications of my reply except Bob. He said, "Then we could be right in the middle of them." He looked me square in the eyes. He still resented me, but he was learning the hard way that there were times in a man's life when he had to forget personal feelings and work for the welfare of all.

He asked the question, so I gave him the answer, man to man. "Looks that way."

Elena caught her breath and closed her eyes. She turned away from us, and her shoulders trembled. I wanted to say something reassuring, to make her feel better, but my tongue had suddenly turned to stone.

Bob laid his hand on her shoulder. "Don't fret like that, Miss Elena. Everything's goin' to work out." He looked back at me, and for a brief moment, the young boy in him surfaced once again. "Won't it?"

All I could do was nod.

We spent the night on the bluff, moving out next morning before sunrise. After the sun rose, I pointed out a ridge of hills to Bob. "See that saddle in those hills?"

Still sullen, he grunted, "Yeah. Why?"

I scooted around and faced him. "You're a man now, Bob. You been doing a man's job the last several days. I don't like to do it, but I'm going to dump a man-sized job on you."

His face paled, but he set his jaw. I continued, "There's Comanche and no telling what else all around us. I got to get out there and find them, find them so we can avoid them. You take the wagon to that saddle in that ridge, you and Miss Elena. I been through this particular part of the state. From here to that saddle is a series of savannahs, grassy meadows with brakes of post oak surrounding them. Stay at the edge of oaks so that if you see anything, you can pull into their shelter. That's about a two day trip, so if I'm not back tonight, find a good spot to bed them down.''

He nodded.

''I'll be gone as long as it takes. It's going to be up to you to handle things here.'' I looked deep into his eyes. He was afraid. Who could blame him? Only a fool wouldn't be, but the determined glint in his eyes showed his grit.

After explaining my plan to Elena, I turned to the children and gave each a job, making each swear to do as Bob said, without argument. Each agreed, although Bernie Taylor tried to balk at taking orders from Bob. I reminded him where I would put my boot if he caused any trouble, and he decided he would be happy to cooperate.

A tiny voice spoke up. ''Mr. Adams?''

It was Rachel. Her bottom lip quivered. She laid her small hand on the goose at her side. ''Are you coming back?''

I reached out and curled my finger under her chin. For once, the goose made no move toward me. ''Don't worry, honey. I'll be back.''

''Be careful, Buster,'' said Elena.

I looked at her. ''I will.''

Swinging into the saddle, I headed northeast, planning on casting out about four, five miles, then swinging back south about ten before turning northeast again—zig-zag like the coyote. That way I could cover a ten-mile-wide corridor through which we were journeying.

The air was clean and fresh, and Hey stepped out smartly, feeling frisky in the late spring weather. The countryside was abloom with reds and yellows and blues. The trees sported new, bright green growth, and the wind, crisp and sweet, blew across my face.

I had always enjoyed traveling alone, laying over when I wanted, taking whatever sidetrips I fancied, doing as I wished. But today, I yearned to be back at the wagon, back with a woman who spoke little, a sullen boy struggling to be a man, four more unpredictable children, and a maniacal goose.

"Wonder why that is, Hey? I haven't fallen lately and hit my head on nothing. My brains aren't scrambled." For the first time in several days, Hey twitched his ears when I spoke. He was finally over being angry with me.

I rode hard, fanning across the Texas countryside, trying to cover as much ground as possible. I ran across sign several times, all of it fresh, all moving south, like some great migration. I had found what I was looking for. Pulling up under a sprawling live oak, I studied the country to the south. Something mighty big must be going on. Whatever it was, I hoped it lasted a few more days, a week, two weeks—long enough to keep the Indians down there while we passed by.

Just before dusk, I spotted feeding deer. I'd forgotten

the last time I'd chewed meat. All we'd been living on had been beans and coffee. A change in our diet would be a welcome treat. I knew I was taking a chance, but I decided the gamble was worth it.

I dropped a fat one with a single shot. I field dressed him quickly, then lashed him behind the cantle and headed north, planning on riding a couple hours into the night before bedding down. If any Indians had heard the shot, they were going to have to work hard for a shot at me.

Using the North Star for bearings and the Big Dipper as a clock, I rode for two hours, then pulled into a cutback along a tiny stream where I made a cold camp.

Moving out early the next morning, I remained deep in the post oak brakes along the grassy savannahs, figuring on intercepting the wagon sometime during the morning. Off to my left was the saddle in the ridge.

When I hadn't found Elena and the kids by midmorning, I grew concerned. By noon, I was alarmed. I shouldn't have left them. Mid-afternoon, I ran across more sign, a broad trail of unshod ponies heading south. Less than a quarter mile farther, I found the trail of the wagon where it had turned north.

Looking around cautiously, I followed the trail through the shadowy brakes, across another small savannah and into another brake. I pulled up and grinned. Ahead, a length of twine was strung across the trail, several inches off the ground. One of George's trip lines.

I looked around for the wagon, but all I saw was a carpet of leaves stretching beneath the canopy of spreading oaks. With a frown, I urged Hey across the line, tripping it, figuring on hearing the noise of pots and pans clattering.

Instead, I heard a noise from the treetops. I looked up just in time to see a five-foot log, suspended at either end by a rope, swooping down at me. "What the . . . " I yelled, throwing myself from the saddle as the log swung past. Hey bolted. I hit the ground and rolled.

From behind me came a clamoring of wild screams. I leaped to my feet just as the three boys burst out from the trees and raced toward me, arms raised, carrying axes, knifes, guns.

When they saw me, they slid to a halt, their eyes wide with stunned surprise. Bob stuttered. "M—Mr. Adams. It . . . It's you. We—I mean, I . . . "

My temper snapped. "You're blasted right, it's me. What's the matter, you blind?" I waved at the log, which had finally stopped swinging. "What the blazes you trying to do, kill me?"

I glared at them. George and Bernie hid behind Bob, only their heads showing. "Was this your idea, George?"

The little boy gulped and nodded. I narrowed my

eyes, and at that moment, considered removing my belt and putting it to a much better use.

Bob spoke up. "We didn't know it was you, Mr. Adams. Honest. We just spotted some Injuns and knew if they found our tracks, they'd follow. We . . . We just decided to make it a little harder on them."

My temper cooled. "This the only one?"

They looked at each other sheepishly. "No, Sir," replied Bernie.

I studied the boys. After all, I was the one who told them to take care of the women. Couldn't fault them for that. I chuckled. "Well, I reckon then you'd better point 'em out to me so I won't walk into one," I replied.

They relaxed and grinned.

By the time we reached the wagon hidden in a small canyon, they had proudly pointed out two more log traps, three snares, and two whip traps. I shook my head and began butchering the deer. "Well, boys. You did a good job. We'll camp here tonight, and then in the morning before we leave, we got to spring all the traps."

George protested. "Yeah, but what if Injuns come along later? We could get some."

I tried to explain my reasoning. "I reckon you have a point there, George, but what if someone like us comes along and gets bad hurt?"

"I sure wouldn't want that to happen," said Bernie. "That ain't nice."

George argued still. "Yeah, but what if it's Injuns . . . some more of them dirty Comanches?"

Bob jumped into the discussion. "Yeah? But what if it ain't? What then?"

Reluctantly, George agreed.

Once again, George set up his trip line around the camp, and we all retired to our respective places.

A short time after midnight, I heard the faint rustling of leaves in the brake. I knew no one could spot me deep in the shadows as I was, so I shifted around and peered into the inky darkness cast by the oaks. Suddenly, I heard a sharp intake of breath followed by the swishing of a falling log. A moment later, a hollow thump like the sound of an Indian drum broke the silence. There was a sharp cry, then nothing.

There came another swishing sound, and another cry. And then the wispy rattle of feet racing over leaves. Another swish, and a startled yelp. I bit my bottom lip to keep from laughing for I could just imagine the confusion of those Comanches stumbling about a forest with logs flying all over the place and snares trying to snap their feet from under them.

Elena and the children slept through it all.

Early next morning as the boys built a small fire, and the girls put coffee and beans on, Bob and I wandered out into the brake. "Have a look," I said, pointing to a puddle of dried blood on the leaves beneath a log trap.

He frowned, then looked up at me in amazement. "Comanche?"

I nodded.

"You mean, they was here last night . . . while we slept?"

"Yep." I pointed to a few other sprung traps. "Looks like you boys did a right good job rigging all these."

Bob grinned like a possum in a henhouse as he hurried to check the other traps. "Here's some more blood," he yelled from one of the whip traps, heavy limbs bent back to be released right into a man's face. "Bet it busted his nose."

Back in camp, the children were ecstatic over Bob's news, but Elena only frowned. "That means they know we're around somewhere," she said out of hearing of the laughing children.

"Afraid so, but one break going our way is that they're all moving south. Something big's going on. Maybe it's big enough that they won't fool around for us. One thing for sure, we can't stay here."

We fried up a batch of venison and moved out, heading for the saddle in the ridge and the Nueces River just beyond. Bernie had been pestering me to ride scout like Bob. Everytime I rode up to the wagon throughout the day, he started up again. Finally, I decided to give him his chance. I put Bob on my pony and Bernie on Bob's. I climbed on the wagon seat and took the reins from Elena, instructing Bernie to ride drag, but remain within a mile of the wagon.

Bob looked at me in disbelief at his own good luck. "You mean . . . you want me . . . me to ride point?"

Point was a critical job. He knew just how important it was. "Why? Don't you think you can do it?"

He cut his eyes toward Elena and squared his shoulders. "Sure, I can. I can do it as good as . . . " He hesitated and glanced at me. He was going to say he could do point as good as me, but he changed his mind. "I can do it as good as anyone," he said, reining Hey around and riding on ahead of us.

"That was nice of you," Elena said, her gaze following Bob.

"I didn't do it to be nice. That one back there," I said, nodding to Bernie, "he's ready to grow up some. He's been trying the last few days. Reckon now's the time to give him the responsibility that'll do it. Besides, we could use some more help."

She arched an eyebrow at me. "You can't fool me. You try to sound gruff, but you're nowhere as hard as you make out. Why, if you were such a hard man, you wouldn't have buried those two Mescaleros you shot back near the river."

I looked at her in disbelief. Then I laughed.

"What's so funny?" she asked, miffed at my laughter.

"You. I didn't bury those Mescaleros out of compassion. I buried them so the buzzards wouldn't find them and point out our location to the other Apaches."

Her mouth dropped open. "You mean . . . " She shivered. "Ugh . . . You mean, you would have just left them lying in the sun . . . that's . . . that's inhuman. Don't you have any feelings at all? I can't believe that's why you buried them."

"That's what I said." Surprised by her reaction, I changed the subject. "You lived out here all your life?"

"Yes. Why?" Her voice was clipped, for my laughter had offended her.

I shook my head. "Your pa must have been a good man and kept you protected mighty well."

She looked up at me, puzzled by my remark. "He was a good man. And yes, he did take care of me, of everyone on the ranch."

"I figured as much, but you see, things out here in the middle of the wilderness, the *despoblado*, are a heap different than back inside the safe walls of a ranch. Out here, a man's got to always keep thinking. You can't give these Indians any opportunity at all. The Comanche, the Apache, the Kiowa, they're all right smart people. You can't sell them short, and sometimes, you've got to do things that you wouldn't otherwise do. Your pa knew that, and you were lucky that he could keep it from you. But one day you'll have to face the truth—if you stay out here.''

She studied me with cold eyes. ''I could never be so unfeeling.'' She jerked around and fixed her eyes on the horses, reining our discussion to a stiff-legged halt.

My ears burned. At that moment, Bob came riding up. Hey had worked up a lather. ''What'd you see out there?'' I asked, still irritated with Elena.

He shook his head. ''Nothing. Why?''

I admit I took my anger at her out on him. ''Then stop riding the horse so hard. Haven't you got any sense? Get off him and get up here on the wagon where you belong.'' Without a backward look, I swung into the saddle and rode away.

Chapter Eight

Whatever big fandango was taking place to the south must have been mighty important, for the number of Indians—Comanche, Mescalero, Apache, Kiowa, Kickapoo, Southern Cheyenne—increased threefold. Several times throughout the day, we were forced to pull into small canyons or thick patches of oak and cedar to await their passing.

The countryside turned more rugged. The wagon bounced and jolted over rocks and small boulders. We crossed the Nueces River and headed for the Frio. Five miles from the Frio River, we were following the rim of a precipitous canyon, the bottom of which was thick with tangles of vines smothering trees, when the iron tire on the front wheel jolted loose and bounced over the edge, disappearing into the green carpet below.

"Can't we still travel?" asked Rachel, pointing to the wheel.

"Not far enough," I replied, more to myself than the others.

"Why not?" asked Bernie. "We still got the wheel." He pointed to the wooden rim on which rode the iron tire.

"Yep. But no wood, not even something strong as Osage orange and white oak, can stand up against the constant pounding against the rocks and boulders." I removed my hat and dragged my forearm across my sweaty brow. "We'll go as far as we can. That's the only choice we got."

"No, it ain't."

Bob stepped forward. "Let's go down and get the tire and bring it back up." He stuck his jaw out. "I'll do it if you're afraid."

Elena's face grew rigid, her eyes wide.

His tone and attitude didn't surprise me. I deserved it after snapping at him about riding Hey too hard. "You take a look at the canyon?"

His brows knit. "No, but—"

I gestured to it. "You best look first. See if you can find a way down."

Giving me a puzzled look, he stepped over to the edge and peered down into the canyon. The walls were sheer, almost three hundred feet. He shook his head. "Don't make any difference. I can go down on a rope and find the wheel. Then we can pull it up, and I'll climb up after it."

"No." I looked at Elena. With my refusal, she had relaxed. "To begin with, you don't know where the tire went. It could be snagged in the top of one of those trees. It could be anywhere. And second, canyons like that, the ground shaded from the sun, are a haven for snakes this time of year." I pointed to the canopy below. "Look."

A long green snake slithered across the canopy and dropped through an opening. "See." The snake was harmless, but I didn't tell him.

He looked around at me, his resolve weakening, but his ego urging him to continue. "I'll look out for them."

"Maybe you would, but the truth is, we can't afford to wait for you. We're out here in the open. We've got to move the wagon, which means we don't have time to waste."

Elena laid her hand on his arm. "Mr. Adams is right, Bob. We must keep moving."

Reluctantly he agreed, and we pushed on, first wrapping the wheel with rope in a last ditch effort to absorb some of the shock.

A mile from the Frio, the front wheel shattered.

"Now what?" asked Elena, staring at the wagon, leaning on its nose.

"Now, we turn Indian," I replied. "We'll right up some travois to carry our supplies." I paused and turned to Rachel. "Will your goose follow, or do we need a string around her neck?"

Rachel nodded. "She'll follow."

We spread the load of blankets, pots, food, canvas top, and tools on three travois, leaving the fourth draft horse for Elena. The girls rode one of the travois. Bernie and George rode the other two.

The heavens opened up just as we reached the Frio. Without the comfort of the wagon, we were forced to rig some shelter. Bob and I used the canvas for a small tent, which did nothing more than funnel the water onto us from a different direction.

While we were struggling to rig the tent, Bernie and George wandered off down river. They returned ten minutes later, running as fast as their legs would carry them. "Mr. Adams! Mr. Adams!"

I grabbed my Winchester as they slid to a muddy halt in front of me. "What is it?"

Bernie pointed down river. "A cave. A big cave."

Elena grinned, and as one, we all reloaded the travois and hurried down river.

The cave was large and dry, the mouth buried behind a thick stand of underbrush. "How did you find it?" I asked.

George shrugged. "We just walked into it."

I grinned. "Well, boys. You did just fine. Just fine."

The rain kept up throughout the night and next morning, but we remained warm and snug in the cave, although the aroma from six wet horses was not redolent of roses. When the rain refused to let up, I decided to take a look outside. Staying warm and dry was indeed a comfort, but keeping our scalps was a sight more important.

I discovered more caves down river, some with access only over rocks and boulders. I backtracked, passing the cave and heading up river. Around a bend two miles distant, I stumbled onto a camp of Kiowa, some thirty or so, huddled around a blazing fire with buffalo robes thrown over their shoulders against the pelting rain.

A bolt of lightning cracked, its discharge deafening to my ears. The Indian ponies reared back against their ropes. While the Kiowa calmed their horses, I hurried back to the cave.

We rigged up and headed out after I explained my plan. We entered the river, then waded downstream to the caves before emerging. Our sign was lost on the rocky banks.

Lighting a couple candles, we moved deep into the cave. Around a sharp bend, the cave opened into a large room, one the size of a barn.

I pulled up. "Here. We wait here." I held the candle out to Bob. "You keep everyone with you."

"Where you going?"

"To wipe out our tracks."

"What about light? Aren't you going to take a candle?" Elena said.

I lit another candle. "I'll be back as soon as I can."

Just inside the entrance of the cave, sand, deposited by a long ago flood, covered a fan-shaped portion of the cave. I erased our sign, then settled down to wait. From where I sat, I could see the underbrush in front of the entrance to the cave in which we had spent the night.

The storm intensified, and as I expected, the band of Kiowas came into view. When they spied the underbrush they halted. A handful disappeared into the underbrush. Moments later, they reappeared and gathered around their chief, gesticulating at the cave and pointing to the ground.

Thunder boomed, and the howling wind hurled thick sheets of rain across the landscape. The chief turned to his followers and indicated the cave, then pointed downstream toward us.

Like a covey of quail, the Kiowa scattered, several disappearing into the underbrush, several more heading our direction. I hurried deep into the cave, avoiding the patches of sand.

Elena and the children sat huddled around the candles, their faces taut with fear. Bob and George stood beside the horses, their hands over the animals' noses.

"We've got to move deeper. The Kiowa are searching the caves for us."

I led the way, deeper and deeper into the rocky earth. Suddenly, we came to a three-way fork. Without hesitation, we headed down the left one. The tunnel angled more to the left, then made a sharp turn and ended in a small room.

My heart jumped into my throat, and I jerked to a halt. Elena bumped into me. "What's wrong?"

"Look." I held the candle out. The flickering light illumined a glistening white skull, its gaping mouth leering at us.

She caught her breath. "Dear Lord."

The children started muttering and pushing forward, curious.

"Quiet," I whispered, my tone harsh.

They stopped. I held the candle over my head, trying to illumine as much of the room as possible. The chamber was a dead end. The only course for us was back, a direction we dared not take, not yet. All we could do was wait. Yet, before us lay a shadowy jumble of various paraphernalia with a sneering skull perched on top.

"Is it dead?" whispered Rachel.

"Dummy. Of course, it is. It's a head," explained Bernie.

A shout echoed down the tunnel.

I spun. "Quick. Against the wall. Don't move. I'll be back." Elena and the boys held the horses, one hand gripping the bridle, the other holding the horse's nostrils. Hey stood silently. I looked at Rachel. "Keep the goose quiet."

The small girl turned to Sally the goose and with her forefinger and thumb pressed together, made a twisting motion like she was turning a key. "Tick-a-lock." She turned back to me and nodded. "Okay, Mr. Adams."

I rolled my eyes.

Hurrying back up the tunnel without the candle, I felt my way to the fork and paused, peering into the solid darkness before me. I heard muffled shouts. Once, a light bounced off the wall some distance before me. For several moments, the glimmer remained steady. After a few minutes, the glow, as the voices, faded.

I waited, the suffocating darkness clinging to me like a second skin, almost taking away my breath. I counted to a hundred, pausing between each count, and then I counted to a hundred again. Finally, I eased forward, one small step at a time.

When I heard the soft rush of the river, I paused. I knew I was staring at the large room just inside the mouth of the cave. I listened for several minutes, but no alien sound disturbed the song of the river. I turned back to the small chamber.

"Are they gone?" Elena looked past my shoulder into the darkness.

"Yeah. We'll stay the night just to be sure."

The children's faces broke into broad grins.

Lowering the candle, I eased forward. Elena and the children followed. "Now let's see what we have over here." The flickering light danced over the grinning skull. A dull reflection bounced off metal. I squatted and stared at the skull. Behind me, the children crowded forward, almost shoving me off my feet. "Stop crowding me," I grumbled.

Bob eased around to one side. "Who was he, do you think?"

"Take a look," I said, picking up a dust-covered breastplace.

"What is it?" asked Elena.

"Spanish armor. Made of dried leather. This fits over his chest and stomach."

"Look at this," shouted George, scrabbling in the thick dust and coming up with a rapier, a slender, two-edged sword with a cup hilt. He swished it once or twice.

"Be careful with that, boy," I demanded. "You'll cut someone."

The skeleton's clothes fell apart at the touch. Bob found a dagger, and in one corner of the room, Bernie discovered a crescent-shaped helmet, the brim of which was turned up front and back. "Look what I found," he shouted, placing the helmet on his head.

Elena spoke up. "What do you think happened to him?"

I glanced at her. The dim, flickering light cast ghostly shadows over her face. "Indians got him, I'd guess. Killed him and then cut off his head."

Rachel shivered. "Why would they do that?"

Bob smirked at her. "Why do you think, silly?" He shook his head. "Boy, you're dumb."

"Oh, shut up. At least—"

Elena cut in. "Hush up, both of you."

Rachel tilted her chin and looked back at me. "Huh?"

I frowned at her. Their spat caused me to forget her first question. "Huh?"

She nodded. "What I asked. Why did they cut off his head?"

I shrugged. "Who knows? From the stories I've heard, when the first Spanish explorers came through here, the Indians were friendly, but after a few years, the white man's diseases and greed turned the natives against him." I nodded to the skull. "Maybe it was a ceremony of some kind, or could be they thought this would keep him wandering in darkness from now on."

Rachel's forehead wrinkled in concentration. "What do you mean, wandering in darkness?"

"The Indian believes that he goes to another world when he dies. There he lives with his father, and his father's father, but if a part of him is missing, he will forever wander the shadows between this world and the Hereafter."

Elena shivered. "Ugh."

Rachel took a step forward and peered curiously at the skelton. "How old do you figure he is?"

"Hard to say. Hundred, maybe two hundred years or so, I'd guess. This kind of armor was what the Spanish wore back in the sixteen hundreds, I think."

George drifted over to the corner of the room and began fencing with an imaginary opponent.

Bob turned the dagger over in his hands, inspecting it. "What did the Spanish people do out here?"

I handed the breast plate to Bernie who tried to fit it over his torso. "Explored. Set up missions."

Rachel walked to the other side of the skeleton, her goose by her side, not uttering a sound. That goose amazed me. She was almost human. "What did they explore for, Mr. Adams?" she asked.

"Gold. Legends claimed gold was everywhere."

Bernie looked up from the breast plate. "Really?"

I laughed. "Not everywhere, not like the stories say, but they did find gold."

"What did they do with it?" asked Bernie.

"Carried it back to Mexico."

"Why?"

"The government wanted it."

Bernie wrinkled his thin face. "Why?"

I glanced at Elena who was grinning at Bernie's barrage of questions. "To help run the country, I reckon."

"I bet it was a lot."

"What they got there was a lot."

He thought a moment. "But—"

"Hush, Bernie," Elena interrupted. "That's enough questions."

Bernie was too engrossed in the gold to quit after only a single reproof. "They didn't get all the gold to Mexico? What did they do with it then?"

"Hid it." I gestured to the room we were in. "In caves like this."

Bernie's eyebrows arched. "You mean, there's gold in this cave."

I grinned at Elena. "No. Not in this one, but maybe in others."

He shook his head. "Boy, I'd sure like to find some." He looked at Elena. "Then we could buy that place like you were talking about, Elena."

She put her arm around his shoulder and hugged him to her. "That'd be nice, Bernie," she said with a sad smile.

Bernie nodded, then looked up at me. "Can I take this armor with me?"

I glanced at Elena. "Sure. Why not?"

Chapter Nine

We pulled out next morning, forded the Frio, and headed southeast for the Medina River. Best I could figure, we were only about seventy or eighty miles from San Antone—four, maybe five days.

The children rode as before, on the horses pulling the travois. Bernie wore his helmet and breastplate. George protested riding a horse with a travois. He wanted to *pretend* with the rapier. When I told him no, he sulked a few moments, then began fighting imaginary opponents, swishing the sword back and forth, chopping off tops of shrubs and small cedars. Bob rode drag. Elena pulled up beside me.

She smiled, her hair damp with perspiration, and

her button nose shiny. "Remind me never to complain about a rough-riding wagon."

I didn't argue.

Suddenly, a faint sound broke the hot, sticky air. I held up my hand. "Hold on."

"What?"

"Listen." I nodded to the rugged terrain ahead of us.

The sound came again, still faint, but I recognized it. "A donkey. That was a donkey braying. Listen."

We all strained to hear. The donkey brayed again.

Elena frowned at me. "Who do you think it is?"

Shaking my head, I pondered the countryside ahead of us. What would a donkey be doing out here? But, why wouldn't one or more be out here? Out in West Texas, camels roamed the desert, the offspring of those desert beasts used in experiments years earlier. The donkey had been the beast of burden throughout Texas for the last two or three centuries. It stood to reason that many of them now ran free.

I indicated a small grove of post oak. "Pull up in those trees. I'll see what's going on up ahead."

Leaving our little party well hidden, I slipped through the post oak and cedar in the direction of the braying donkey. Half-a-mile out, I ran across a set of wagon tracks in the damp soil, a wagon pulled by a single donkey. One glance at the wheel tracks, and I knew what I would find ahead.

The terrain rose to a small hill topped with cedar

and prickly pear. I crouched behind a twisted cedar and peered into the valley below.

There stood the braying donkey, harnessed to a small *carreta*, a small two-wheeled cart, one of which lay on the ground. Next to the wooden wheel sprawled a man wearing the traditional white cotton *camisa* and *pantalones* of the Mexican peon. He lay without movement.

I looked around, studied the far side of the valley as well as each hiding place within half-a-mile, but I saw nothing out of the ordinary.

Taking a deep breath, I slipped from behind the cedar and ghosted down the gentle slope, darting from tree to tree, shrub to shrub until I was within a few feet of the peon.

I called out to the supine man. "Hey!"

The donkey stopped braying and looked around, but the man did not move.

I called again. No movement came from the man.

Glancing around once again, I turned my attention back to the inert figure sprawled on his back. The wind had blown his baggy *camisa* over his head, revealing a bare mid-section. The lower portion of his torso was dark, much darker than the flesh above.

He was dead. Of that I was certain. I'd seen enough dead men to recognize the signs. While I don't know what causes it, I know that when a man dies, that part of his body closest to the ground turns much darker.

I looked over my shoulder, searched the hills rimming the small valley, and then hurried to the dead man. Pulling his shirt from his face, I grimaced at the agony on his rigid face. Looking over the body, I saw no wounds, no injuries, no sign of violence.

Wasting no time, I pulled him next to a large boulder and covered him with rocks, draping the cross he wore about his neck on a broken branch I placed at his head for a marker.

Propping the axle on rocks, I groaned to lift the heavy wooden wheel and slide it into place. I fashioned a wooden pin and hammered it into the axle to hold the wheel in place, the absence of which had precipitated the loss of the wheel.

The donkey was a small jinny, tough as a dried mesquite post, gentle as a kitten. Leading the jinny, I headed back to Elena and the children.

Elena appraised the cart with distrust as we transferred the load, keeping only the axe and leaving behind the other tools. I tried to hitch a draft horse to the cart, but the shafts were too short, and the large animal's hooves struck the *carreta*, so we left the donkey in the traces.

Elena and the girls opted to ride in the cart, while George and Bernie now each had his own horse. The other two we tied to the cart. Bob rode drag, and I, once again, rode point.

The day passed slowly. George roamed far and wide on his horse, engrossed in slaying bushes and shrubs with his sword, I was constantly calling him back in until I threatened to put him in the cart with the girls.

"Aw, but Mr. Adams, I got to protect the wagon train." With that, he took another vicious swipe at a dried mesquite pod.

I glanced at Elena who was smiling at me. I just shook my head and rode back to point. The sun beat down. Before an hour passed, Bernie slipped out of the breastplate and helmet and deposited them in the *carreta*.

The second day began as the first with Bob at drag and me at point. At noon we pulled into the shade of an arbor of post oak beside a small stream to eat a bite and rest an hour or so. While we nooned, I glanced around the camp. "Where's George?"

"I think he's on the other side of the cart," Bob replied. He called out. "George? You over there?"

"No. He ain't over here," Bernie yelled back.

Elena, who had been lying on a blanket in the shade sat upright. "George? George? Where are you?"

There was no answer.

I grimaced and slammed my fist into the palm of my hand. "Where in the blazes did that knot-headed boy go?" I shouted. That's all I needed, another day lost.

Bob stood staring at me, his eyes wide, his face taut with concern. "Where do you think he is?"

I threw up my hands in a gesture of futility. "How should I know. He went plumb crazy with that sword. For all I know, he cut down a tree, and it fell on him."

"Buster! Don't say that! He could be hurt."

I jerked around at Elena's outburst. My ears were burning. I wanted to lash out at someone, at something, but the concern etched on her face shamed me. I tried to erase some of her fears. "He's all right. He probably just got busy playing his games and wasn't paying any attention to us." I nodded to our backtrail. "He's probably following our tracks now."

She forced a faint smile. "I hope so."

"Don't worry. I'll go back for him." I shook my head and turned to Bob. "Load 'em up, Bob." I pointed to the southeast. "Head that direction. I'll find that redheaded little scamp and follow your trail. If I'm not back before dark, you take care of things, you hear?"

He nodded and licked his lips. He gulped. "I hear."

I studied him a moment. I couldn't tell if he'd grown up much in the last few days or not. He was still sullen. "Good."

"Here." Elena handed me a canteen and an oilcloth full of corndodgers.

I turned for my pony, but Bob stopped me. "And . . . And you don't have to worry about nothing. I'll do just like you would."

A grin ticked up the side of my mouth. "That's good enough." I surveyed the entire party. "Now who saw him last?"

Mary ignored us. She just kept writing in that small diary of hers.

Sifting through the information, Rachel was the last to see George, about four miles back when we made a turn to the east. He had dismounted his horse and was swinging on a vine hanging from some large oaks. "You know, just before we crossed that little creek. He was in the trees across the meadow with that sword of his."

Clicking my tongue, I urged Hey into a running walk. Behind me the *carreta* rumbled and groaned as Bob headed them on toward the Medina River.

All my life, I had ridden by myself. I grew up alone, no family. I came to enjoy the solitude of the vast, sprawling country that was Texas. My entertainment was the yelping coyote, the feeding deer, the swooping hawk. They had once been sufficient, but now a strange emptiness filled me, puzzled me.

I turned in the saddle and looked over my shoulder in the direction of Elena and the children. An uncomfortable longing to be back among them settled in my chest. I studied over the strange feeling. It was an emotion I had never before encountered, and I wasn't quite certain how I felt about it.

An hour later, I pulled up at the small creek and scanned the stand of oaks across a broad savannah, the grassy area Rachel had called a meadow. There was no movement, but I did spot the hanging vines of which Rachel had spoken.

And beneath the vines, I found George's tracks. I

reined Hey around and followed the boy's trail. I had been right. From the many fresh scars on the trunks of the rugged oaks, George must have had himself a mighty battle with desperate foes.

I shook my head, grinning, despite my impatience with the boy-imp. He needed a good tanning, but I did admire his imagination.

Abruptly, I pulled up and stared at the ground in surprise. Hoof prints! Unshod hoof prints. I shucked my .44 and quickly scanned the area. There was no movement, no sign of Indians. I leaned from the saddle for a better look.

Best I could figure, there were four ponies, and the tracks were still fresh. Even from where I was sitting, I could see the damp had not dried from the bottom of the overturned leaves. My heart thudded against my chest. The trail was fresh. Ten, maybe fifteen minutes.

The backtrail of the Indians led to the south. Could whatever had drawn so many warriors in that direction have concluded? Were all the Indians headed back north? I hoped not.

Their tracks paralleled George's trail, obviously following it. Slowly, I trailed both sets, my eyes never still. I studied every stem of grass, every rock, every tree.

At the base of one tree, the leaves were pressed down and the ground disturbed by heel marks. From the sign,

George must have sat and leaned against the tree. I studied the sign.

George must have dozed off, and the approach of the Indians had awakened him. He scrambled to his feet and, from the length of his stride, he broke into a run.

The Indians gave chase. George didn't have a chance for some distance from the tree, his tracks suddenly vanished. The pony sign on either side indicated two Indians had swooped down and picked him up by his arms.

Following slowly, I tagged after the Indians, who, for some reason, headed southeast, parallel with our own route. "Whoa, boy," I muttered to Hey, tugging on the reins. "Let's you and me give them time to get a little ahead of us."

Dismounting, I loosened the cinch and poured some water in my hat for Hey, after which I took a long drink from the canteen. I figured on snaking up on them after dark. Then I would play it all by ear.

Fifteen minutes later, I set out on their trail. I kept hoping they wouldn't cut back north. If they did, they would run across the *carreta's* tracks.

As the sun dropped below the horizon, I pulled into a thicket of cedar at the base of a rocky bluff. Tying Hey, I climbed the bluff and surveyed the country below. Off to my right in the middle of a post oak brake, a fire winked in the growing dusk. A couple miles, I guessed.

Quickly, before the light faded, I tried to pick out a route to the fire. Tracing the edge of the post oak brake along the savannah, I noted a stand of oak in the middle of the lush grassland.

From where I stood, the stand of oak appeared due north of the fire. At least I had a jumping off spot.

Upon reaching the stand, I cut south, tying Hey just inside the line of oak rimming the savannah. Pulling my Winchester from its boot, I headed toward the fire. The leaves still contained some moisture from the storm, so I was able to keep noise to a minimum.

Thirty minutes later, I spotted the flicker of the fire through the trees. Pressing against the rugged bark of an oak, I studied the fire. Shadows moved in front of it.

I tested the wind. Very little. That bothered me.

Strong winds tore headlong through a brake, un-deterred by the snarl of leaves and branches; but gentle breezes were unpredictable, their currents twisted and tangled by the same snarl of branches.

Trying to keep the wispy drifts of air in my face, I eased toward the camp. Indian ponies seemed to have an unusually keen sense of smell, especially for the white man. For George's sake, I couldn't afford to be discovered, so I moved carefully.

I grinned when the rich aroma of broiling venison reached my nostrils. The mixture of meat and woods-moke would overpower my own scent. I moved closer, taking sanctuary behind a fallen tree less than a hundred feet from the fire.

Four Comanches squatted around the fire, staring at the haunches of broiling meat. One wore two feathers, the sign of a young, ambitious warrior. Beyond them sat George, leaning against an oak, his eyes fixed on his captors. In the dim light at such a distance, his features were hard to discern. His slender face seemed more pale, but he wasn't crying—and that made me mighty proud.

Glancing over my shoulder, I wondered if any other Comanches were nearby. Or was this party just what it appeared, a small band of warriors returning to its village?

I laid my hand on the butt of my sixgun. My fingers settled naturally around the smooth walnut grips. I could kill all four before they had a chance to move, but no telling who or what the shots would bring. Best to take care of it without any sound or disturbance.

I pulled back into the darkness and waited. No sooner had I settled in behind an ancient oak than a nightbird called from the darkness.

The four Comanches jumped to their feet, cocking their Brass Boy Winchesters and battered Springfields.

Chapter Ten

The Comanches lowered their rifles as six more warriors rode into camp. The warrior with the two feathers raised his hand and spoke to the newcomers.

Taking advantage of the commotion their arrival created, I slipped in closer once again, hoping to learn anything that would help me rescue George.

"Come. Eat," said Two Feathers, pointing to the venison.

Dismounting, the Comanches sliced slabs from the broiling haunches and gulped the meat, washing it down with water from their jugs.

One newcomer rose and pointed to George.

Two Feathers replied, gesturing to their backtrail

where they had captured the young boy. "He is without family. We find him along the trail."

The newcomer, his face hard with anger, grunted and stalked over to George who rose to face him.

I slid the muzzle of the Winchester through a tangle of undergrowth and centered the sights in the middle of the newcomer's back. I cocked the hammer. Both George and me were dead if I had to fire, but I couldn't let the big Comanche hurt the boy. I kept my eyes on the warrior's hand. The moment he pulled his knife, I would fire.

But he didn't reach for his knife. He glared down at George who tried to return the look. Newcomer reached out and gave George a hard shove.

The boy stumbled back and banged his head against the oak. Instantly, arms and legs windmilling, he tore into the Comanche warrior, beating the brave on the chest.

At first shocked by the boy's attack, the warrior then laughed and grabbed George under his arms and lifted him over his head, shouting to the other warriors. "Ho. See what we have. A young badger. He thinks to take coup on Man of Horses."

George stopped fighting, staring down at the laughing Indian in surprise. He glanced around the band of Indians, all laughing with Man of Horses.

Man of Horses said, "This one, he will make good

Comanche.'' He lowered George to the ground. "He will ride with us. He will be a great warrior." The Comanche leader rose to his full stature and stared down at the boy. "Come." He indicated the fire. "Fill your stomach. Then sleep well. We ride before the sun brings another day."

Though puzzled and frightened, George obeyed. He was bright enough to realize the advantages of being accepted by the Comanche.

I slipped back into the night, wishing there was some way to let the young boy know he wasn't alone, but I dared not take any chances. I would follow and wait, and hope I could take advantage of the opportunity to rescue him when it arose.

During the night another rain storm, filled with rumbling thunder and exploding lightning, swept through—a fierce downpour that removed one of my concerns by erasing the tracks of the *carreta*.

The Comanche warriors pulled their buffalo robes over their heads and continued sleeping as the severe weather struck, leaving only one warrior to watch the ponies, to keep them calm.

I figured this was my chance. If I could stampede the ponies, the warriors would have to give pursuit, and provide me with the opportunity to rescue George.

Lightning cracked, illumining the brake in eerie relief. Crouching, I slipped through the darkness to the horses. The frightened animals reared and pawed at the dark sky. Lightning snapped, and the Comanche sentry stood with his rain-wet back to me, his arms raised to calm the horses.

I rose quickly and, grabbing the butt of my Winchester with both hands, swung it like a club, slamming the muzzle against his temple. He fell like a sack of oats. I looked over my shoulder to see George, sitting up, a soaking blanket over his shoulders, watching me. I motioned him into the woods, and then cut the ropes holding the ponies.

I fired two shots into the night and hightailed it for George.

The camp exploded to life. Shouts and warwhoops echoed in counterpoint to the booming thunder and sizzling lightning. I found George crouching behind a tree a hundred feet from camp.

Grabbing his hand, we cut north. "What's that in your hand?" I yelled.

"My sword. I ain't leaving it behind."

I muttered to myself.

Behind us came a din of angry cries.

Suddenly, the pounding of hooves thundered above the roar of the storm.

We angled away from the sound of hoofbeats. Another hundred feet and the ground gave way under our feet. We stumbled and went tumbling to the ground, scattering the thick layer of leaves.

In the next burst of lightning, I saw that we had

stumbled into a shallow depression, like a bowl. "Quick. Over there," I said, pushing George toward a fallen tree at the edge of the basin. "On the ground."

He fell to the ground beside the tree, and I covered him with leaves, after which I lay beside him and pulled leaves over me. I hoped we would escape detection in the darkness.

Short seconds later, voices called from the darkness around us. On several occasions, horses came within scant feet of us. Each time, I flexed my fingers on the grip of the rifle butt, ready to leap to my feet if necessary.

Soon the storm passed.

I dreaded the coming of day, and the search by the Comanche. Our position was secure during the night, but with the rising of the sun, they would find us easily. I laid my hand on George's arm.

"What?" he whispered.

"Let's go. Hands and knees, and be real quiet."

Voices still sounded from the darkness around us. We crept from tree to tree until finally, the search fell behind. When their voices became distant, we rose to a crouch and hurried northward, hoping on striking the savannah so I could get my bearings.

George stayed right behind me, never complaining once. His breathing became labored, so I slowed my pace. I lost track of time, and before I realized it, the sky to the east was growing lighter. In the next instant, we reached the savannah.

"Hold it," I whispered, pulling up.

George stumbled and fell into me. I held him up. "You okay, son?"

Gasping for breath, he nodded, his pale face like a mask in the darkness.

I squeezed his arm. "Good."

From over my shoulder, a whinney cut through the early morning. "It's Hey," I muttered. "Let's go."

George tried to follow, but he stumbled and sprawled on the ground. He was exhausted.

Squatting, I picked him up in my arms.

"My sword. Where's my sword?"

"Forget it," I replied, hurrying to the waiting horse.

He squirmed in my arms. "No. I want my sword."

For a moment, I glared at him, then I relented. I'd spend more time arguing with him than I would handing him the blasted sword. "Okay, okay." I sat him on the horse's croup. "Just be quiet."

I ran back to where he had fallen and retrieved the sword.

He stuck it under his belt, and I swung into the saddle. "Hold on to me," I said, pulling Hey around and breaking across the savannah.

I didn't dare head after Elena and Bob, not with the Comanches behind. If they found my sign on the savannah, they would follow. My best bet was to try to lose them. I headed for the small creek winding its way across the grassy plains.

We splashed into the creek and turned upstream, taking advantage of the rocky bed. The Comanche were skilled trackers, and I would no more bet on losing them than I would on drawing to an inside straight flush. But we had to try.

The sun rose over the rugged hills. A light mist hung over the countryside, settling in the valleys and between the hills.

"Whoa, boy," I said, pulling up and staring at the stream bank on my right. It was sandy, but beyond the sand, a talus of rock ascended to a bluff.

Glancing over my shoulder, I shrugged. If my trick didn't work, we were no worse off than we were now. I headed Hey across the sand and onto the talus wet with the mist. We rode forward a hundred feet or so and halted.

Off to my left the creek curled back to the northwest. I grinned. The ground between us and the creek was a rocky plate. I turned Hey across the plate. When we reached the stream, I dismounted and gave the reins to George. "I'll be back."

Staying on the rocks, I clambered to the top of the bluff, where I deliberately broke a few small limbs on some cedars. A few feet farther, I dropped a cartridge. "I don't know," I muttered. "At least it's a chance."

Returning to Hey and George, I climbed into the

saddle, and we followed the stream into a narrow canyon thick with mist. The sunlight shimmered off the tiny globules of water suspended in the air around us. I felt George shiver.

I pulled up, studying the stream banks. Here, they were sheets of rock, one on top of the other, like clapboard, still wet from the mist. Riding farther, I halted at the first oak leaning over the stream and broke a twig. We backtracked then and left the stream on the rocky plates. With luck, any marks we left on the rocks would be washed away by the fog. "Hold on, George. We're going out."

Clambering up the bank, we followed a rocky wash leading to the top of one of the small bluffs that formed the canyon. On top, we broke out of the mist. Before us lay more rugged country, canyons choked with oa' and cedar. I kicked Hey in the flanks. "Let's go, b¢ Put the miles behind."

George still had his arms wrapped around me head pressed against my back. "You all righ' there, George?"

He dragged in a deep breath. "Yes, sir, Mr Just tired."

"We'll stop directly. First we need sor between us."

I had planned to ride longer, but fifteen I felt his grip loosening about my wai sagging against my back. He was ex'

Pulling Hey back into a walk, I looked over the country around us. All three of us could do with some rest. Gently, I slapped the back of George's hands. "Hold on, boy. We're going to stop as soon as I find a place."

"Yes, sir," he muttered.

A few minutes later, we pulled into a thick stand of cedar high on a bluff overlooking the country behind us. In the distance, about a mile, I guess, the small stream wound across the savannah.

"We'll rest here awhile."

The thin-faced boy nodded and slid from the horse.

Dismounting, I unbuckled the cinch and pulled the saddle from Hey, an act taking no more than fifteen seconds. When I turned around, George had curled on his side at the base of a small cedar, sleeping, his cheek resting on his folded hands. His sword lay by his side.

I pulled my blanket from my soogan and spread it over the boy. With my tarp, I rigged a fly to keep the sun off of George. Afterward, taking my Winchester and canteen along with a handful of corndodgers, I found a spot overlooking our backtrail, an opening in the midst of small cedars that permitted me a panoramic view of our backtrail.

The sleepless night caught up with me. I fought against sleep as hard as I could, shaking my head, slapping my face, even pouring water over my head,

but nothing helped. Each time, within moments, I'd find myself nodding again.

I leaned back against the oak and stared at the sun through the canopy of leaves. I closed my eyes. It felt like heaven.

Later, how much later I don't know, I jerked awake, a crick in my neck. Alarmed, I shook my head to clear the fog and looked around. My heart jumped into my throat.

The sun was high overhead, and the mist had burned away.

In the middle of the savannah, half-a-dozen Comanche rode single file, following the stream. Had they found our sign? I slipped to the other side of my sanctuary so I could keep an eye on them as they drew near the false trail I laid up the side of the rock-strewn bluff.

Behind me, George slept peacefully. I envied him. Sleeping without a care. But then, I felt a little proud of myself for I suddenly realized I was the reason George could sleep so soundly.

I stretched out on my belly beneath the boughs of a small cedar near the edge of the bluff. The Comanche were still a considerable distance from the first false trail. I drew a deep breath and waited.

Time dragged. I wondered about Elena and the children. Bob could take care of them, I told myself. He'd grown up a lot, although he still resented me. That was okay. A lot of young men on the verge of growing up resent their pa's, just like young girls and their ma's always seem to be arguing.

I looked around at George, wondering how I would feel if I had them all on my place near Bastrop. The bottom land near the Colorado River was deep and rich, capable of growing any crop a jasper planted. Game was plentiful, and the family larder would always be well-stocked.

And Bastrop was becoming civilized. A few renegade Indians passed by on occasion as well as hombres trying to make a name for themselves with their guns, but for the most part, churches and schools had come to stay.

A tinge of guilt burned my cheeks when I thought of Natalia Ludden, fair-complected, used to the good things in life. How would she take to these five children? I didn't want to admit it, but I knew she wouldn't approve of them.

The clatter of hoofs jerked me from my reverie. In the distance, the first Comanche had stopped and was staring at the tracks I had left in the sand. Another warrior pulled up beside him, and for a few moments, they spoke, gesticulating at the ground.

One barked some commands to the others, and three braves urged their ponies up the slope of talus while those who remained behind studied the canyons and hills around them. Instinctively, I ducked even though I knew they could not see me.

Peering through the branches of the cedar, I watched as one of the Comanches on the bluff waved to those below and held up his hand. He was too far to discern what he held, but I knew it was the cartridge.

The other four climbed the hill and disappeared into the oak and cedar beyond.

Sighing with relief, I laid my head on my forearm and closed my eyes. The smartest move on our part was to sit tight. Let them search, then move out after dark.

My eyelids sagged with sleep. How I wished for one of George's traps. Somehow, I managed to remain awake until midafternoon when I awakened George.

He drank half the canteen of water and gobbled down the rest of the corndodgers.

"I'm going to take a short nap. Wake me just before sundown."

He nodded. "Yes, sir."

"And stay awake," I said, shaking my finger at him.

George grinned and waved his sword over his head. "Don't worry about nothing, Mr. Adams. I'll keep good watch."

He shook me awake just as the sun rolled behind the horizon. "It's time, Mr. Adams. Sundown."

I blinked my eyes and sat up. "See anything?" I mumbled.

"No, sir. Nothing. Not a thing."

"No sign of Comanche?"

"No, sir."

"Good." I poured water in my hand and splashed it on my face, after which I took a long drink from the canteen. I rose to my feet. "I reckon it's time to get started." Staring out over the rapidly darkening countryside, I figured on backtracking a couple miles, then cutting southeast.

Saddling Hey, I helped George up behind the saddle and then swung aboard. Slowly, we made our way down the hill, trying to stay away from the rocks, an impossible task. Hey's shod hooves clattered on the rocks, the sound of which carried in the still night air.

Several times before we reached the base of the hill, I pulled up beside a cedar or oak and listened. The only sounds were those of the night.

Finally we rode onto the savannah. I glanced to the east. The waning moon would rise in about thirty minutes. If we rode hard, we would have a couple miles behind us by the time it rose.

"Hold on, boy. This is going to be rough." I urged Hey into a gallop. His long legs reached out and gathered in the ground. The savannah sped past. I felt George grow tense as he tightened his legs about the animal's croup and belly.

Like ghosts, we fled through the night, a dark shadow gliding across a black landscape. Far to our right, the oaks rimming the savannah appeared as an obscure line, blotting out the stars on the horizon. To our left, a row of pale hills rose into the night sky, the rocks and boulders gray bones in the darkness.

A thin crescent rose beyond the horizon. I pulled Hey closer to the hills on my left.

Suddenly, a bulky shadow erupted from a patch of cedar and slammed into us, sending us spinning to the ground. Before I could leap to my feet, a body landed on me. I looked up to see the starlight bounce off an upraised tomahawk.

Chapter Eleven

I jerked my head aside at the last second. The iron blade grazed my ear. I rolled to my left, swinging my doubled arm with all my strength. The point of my elbow caught my assailant on the side of the head, slamming him aside. I rolled back to my right and jumped to my feet, my hand flashing to my sixgun in the same motion. I grabbed empty leather.

With a cry, the Indian leaped at me, swinging his tomahawk in a horizontal loop at my head. I ducked, pulling my knife, a six inch blade with a razor edge. In the same motion, I struck out with the knife, opening a shallow cut along his ribs. I was no knife fighter, but I knew how to take care of myself.

The dim glow from the stars and waning moon

touched his prominent cheekbones and lips with a pale blue glow. His eyes were lost in dark sockets, but his lips were twisted in surprise.

From the corner of my eye, I saw movement. "Get the horse, George. Now."

The Comanche made a move toward George, but I stepped in front of him, waving the tip of my blade. "You go through me first, friend," I said, knowing he couldn't understand me.

He grunted and dropped back into a crouch, circling to my left and feinting with his weapon. Abruptly, he charged, swinging in a downward blow.

I parried his blow with my knife, but the impact sent my blade spinning. The Comanche jumped back around, a smug grin on his face. He yelled and charged again.

Timing his swing, I grabbed his wrist with one hand and his hair with the other and fell backward, jamming my feet in his stomach and flipping him onto his back. I jumped to my feet and kicked the tomahawk from his hand.

He stumbled to his feet, dazed. I stepped forward and threw a right cross at the point of his chin. His head snapped around, and I swung a left from my knees. I popped his head back, and he fell like a tree.

I stood unmoving for several seconds, my chest heaving and sweat stinging my eyes. I heard George come up and stop behind me. "You all right, boy?"

"Y . . . Yes, sir."

I retrieved my hat and sixgun and studied the Indian pony, which looked like he just might fit in the harness in place of the donkey. "You know how to ride bareback?"

George grinned. "My pa taught me good."

The Indian pony stood ground-reined, watching us curiously. I hooked my thumb at him. "He's yours."

The boy nodded eagerly and, speaking softly, approached the small pony. The pony nickered and took a step backward, but George calmed him. He whispered to the pony a few more seconds, then turned to me. "Can you help me up?"

I grinned and gave him a hand, half expecting the pony to pitch with the boy, but the animal stood motionless while George leaned forward and patted his neck.

Arching an eyebrow at the boy's knack with the pony, I knelt and quickly bound and gagged the unconscious Comanche for his friends to later discover. I don't like killing of any kind, though I've done more than my share, but if I can avoid it, I do.

Knowing we would be followed, I cut due south, crossing the savannah and disappearing into the post oak brake, twisting and turning through thickets, along gullies, around the edges of small ponds. Such deception was time consuming, but I could not take a chance on leading the Comanches to Elena and the children.

Slowly we worked back to the north, crossing the savannah and riding back into the rugged canyons and craggy hills. By evening, we had made a wide swing across the rough countryside and made camp near the crest of the tallest hill around.

I handed the canteen to George. "Drink your fill, son. That's all we got. If we don't spot the Comanche trailing us, come morning, we'll get us some fresh meat and take time to cook it up."

George patted his stomach. "Sounds awful good to me, Mr. Adams."

While there was still enough light to see, I set several traps along rabbit trails, hoping to get lucky.

We spotted no Comanche that night.

And we got lucky, for a small cottontail was snagged in our first trap. I quickly field dressed it, and we headed down into the canyons, hoping to find a thick canopy of leaves to dissipate smoke from our small fire.

An hour later, we rode back to the savannah and headed southeast, our bellies full. Now we had to catch Elena and Bob who would be at the Medina River by now.

Bernie had told the truth about George's knack with horses. The youngster stayed right up with me. He forked that Comanche mustang just like he was growed to it. A little feller like that could be a mighty big help on my ranch near Bastrop.

But no sooner did the thought hit me than I remembered Natalia, and for the first time since I had known her, I felt a nudge of resentment toward her. And that feeling puzzled me.

To me, a loner struggling to build something grand out of my rawhide and green stick ranch, Natalia Ludden was unattainable. Then she smiled at me. I could have jumped a twelve-foot fence and kicked my heels together. She was the prettiest, the most charming, the best educated, the most citified woman I had ever met, and when she deigned me permission to court her, I figured I had died and gone to a special kind of heaven.

That's why the feelings nagging at me were so puzzling. I tried to shove them aside, to hide them in a little room in my mind and shut the door, but they kept opening the door, and I'd shove them back—and it started all over again until I figured to just let them wander around in my head until they got tired, and then maybe they'd go back to that little room on their own.

I glanced at George. He was glued to that pony, a big grin on his face. The wind whipped his red hair, and he reminded me of myself when I was his age. Of course that was back in the olden days, when things were really rough out here on the frontier.

Late in the afternoon, we found Elena and the children's sign in a stand of cedar. ''Bob moved them a good piece before the rain,'' I said, glancing over my shoulder.

George frowned up at me. ''Why do you say that, Mr. Adams?''

I removed my hat and dragged my arm across my forehead to wipe away the sweat. ''I mean, this is where they camped the night we escaped from the Comanches.'' I nodded ahead. ''We'll follow their trail a few more miles before we bed down. How does that sound?''

Before George could reply, his stomach growled. He ducked his head. ''Sorry.''

I realized then we had not eaten since morning. I was used to it, but George wasn't. ''Tell you what. If I remember right, up ahead is a small stream. Let's stop there, and I'll show you how the Indians down on the Gulf of Mexico catch fish. Sound okay to you?''

A big grin popped on his face. ''Yes, sir. It sure does.''

At the small creek, we tied our horses in some browse beneath a large willow. I loosened Hey's cinch. He might as well be comfortable, but if we had to ride out in a hurry, I didn't want to take time to throw the saddle back on.

''How are you goin' to catch the fish, Mr. Adams?''

I winked at him. ''Watch. Once I lived with Atta-pacas down on the coast, and this is how they did it.

Pay attention. It might come in handy for you some-day.''

He nodded and sidled closer while I searched the willow for the right limb. I found one about as big around as a shotgun barrel and twice as long.

Using my knife, I split one end about eight inches and then carved teeth like a jack-o-lantern on the inside. At the base of the split, I wrapped rawhide around the limb to keep the branch from splitting ever farther. Then I opened the mouth wide and inserted a twig to keep it open. I held it out to George.

He took it in his hands and studied it. ''How does it work?''

I pointed to the twig holding the gaping mouth open. ''Kinda like a spear. That's what the Attacapa called it, a fish spear. When you bend the two pieces of the limb apart, they want to spring back. This twig keeps them apart. When you jam this mouth down over a fish, the twig breaks and the two pieces of the limb snap together. The teeth hold the fish until you can get him out.''

George turned it over in his hands and whistled while I tied another piece of rawhide to the middle of a small branch a few inches long. ''Does it really work?'' He patted the hilt of his sword. ''Couldn't I get them with this?''

''Maybe. You can try.''

He considered it, but the fish spear was too attractive. "Maybe later."

"Watch." I took it from him. "Take off your shoes." I removed my boots and together, we waded into the creek. "We'll ease upstream." I handed him the rawhide tied to the small branch.

"What's this for?"

"A stringer. You need something to put your fish on, don't you?"

He grinned up at me. "If we catch any," he said, his grin growing wider.

I arched an eyebrow. "Don't worry. We will." At that moment, Natalia was coming in a poor second to this red-headed little urchin with the big grin on his face.

"Where are the fish?" he whispered.

"See all those rocks and boulders sticking out of the water?"

"Yes."

"Now, look at the current. See how it swirls behind the rocks?"

"Yes, sir."

"That's where the fish are waiting. The current brings bugs down, and when they swirl about the rocks, Mr. Fish is waiting. Now follow me, but don't splash."

We eased forward. I stopped and pointed to the water swirling behind a large rock. A dim, wavering shadow lay behind the rock. I looked down at George.

He nodded, his eyes fixed on the fish.

Keeping the spear under water, I eased it slowly toward the fish. George crowded right up behind me, curious as a young kitten. I poised the spear over the fish, and then suddenly, lunged downward, holding the struggling fish to the bed until I could get my fingers in its gill.

"Here you are," I said, holding up a fat bass. "Now are you convinced it works?"

He bobbed his head energetically. "Yes, sir. Yes, sir. Can I try it, huh? Can I?"

"Sure you can." I handed him the spear and strung the bass on the stringer. "Get another twig to hold it open, then go ahead, but move slow. Don't spook the fish."

George missed the first three or four before he found the knack. Then he tried his best to deplete the creek of fish. I had to explain to him that even if he was starving, he couldn't eat all the fish he wanted to catch, and besides, he didn't want to injure a fish just for sport.

We returned to the horses with four fat fish, two bass and two perch. I was tired, and George was excited, not a good combination. "Can I fish after we eat?"

"We don't need the fish, George."

He stared at me, and I could see the wheels turning

in his head. Suddenly, his eyes lit up. "What about in the morning? We got to eat breakfast."

"We'll be pulling out before sunrise. You can't see the fish in the dark."

He studied me a few more seconds. "Why couldn't I catch them while supper is cooking and put them on the stringer and leave them in the creek overnight?"

I took a deep breath and released it slowly. He had me there. "Why don't you go right ahead and do that, George. Sounds like a good idea to me."

With a gleeful whoop, he was back in the creek in two steps.

By the time the sun rose, we were three miles from camp, our bellies full and our spirits high. The *carreta* tracks led us through small streams, across lush valleys, down winding canyons, and over rugged hills. A beautiful country, it reminded me of my place back in Bastrop.

Just before dark, we reached the Medina River where the *carreta* tracks abruptly ended without entering the river.

We reined up.

George looked up at me. "Where did they go?"

I shook my head and looked around. "I don't know. They just vanished."

Chapter Twelve

I knew they couldn't have just up and vanished, but the sudden disappearance of their sign on the sandy bank was mighty puzzling. Dismounting, I knelt and studied the ground. A few feet up river, the sandy bank gave way to rock, and that's were I found a track in a shallow basin of sand.

Sitting back on my heels, I grinned up at George. "They're getting sneaky on us."

"What do you mean?"

"Take a look." I nodded to the faint sign in the sand gathered in the small depressions on the rocky plate. "They wiped out their tracks over there and headed up this way." I rose and peered into the un-

140

dergrowth up river, wondering why they had taken so much pain to cover their tracks.

"You reckon they was trying to give the slip to some Comanche?"

That made sense to me, but I had seen no sign throughout the day. "Could be." Leading Hey, I walked up river, studying the rocky bank. Another track.

Then the faint trail took a peculiar turn back to the northwest, into a rocky crag of towering bluffs choked with shin oak, mesquite, and cedar. A shallow creek ran out of the canyon into the Medina.

We wound our way back into the canyon. "Hold it."

George pulled up beside me. I pointed to the ground ahead of us, and a big grin bloomed on his face. "My trap," he whispered. We stared at the length of twine camouflaged by small branches and leaves.

"Yep. They did a purty good job too."

Looking beyond the trip line, I spotted a thick patch of oak. That's probably where they had forted up. I cupped my hand to my mouth. "Anyone there?"

No answer.

I called again. Still no answer.

Dismounting, I handed the reins to George. "Wait here."

Stepping over the trip line, I unleathered my .44 and

crept through the mesquite and oak into the patch of tall oak. I froze beside the trunk of a gnarled oak. Directly ahead sat the *carreta*. The donkey, still in harness, looked back at me with sad eyes. A cold chill ran up my spine.

If anything had happened to them, I'd—

"Mr. Adams, Mr. Adams!"

I looked around to see Rachel, followed by the squawking goose, bounding through a tangle of berry vines toward me, their faces bright glee. George was right behind me on the small pony. Rachel jumped on me, almost knocking me off my feet.

"Whoa, there," I said, laughing, but keeping my eyes on the crazy goose who had pulled up and was eyeing me with beady eyes.

She bubbled with happiness, her words gushing in a tangle of confusion thicker than the berry briars through which she had just run.

Beyond them, Bob and Elena crashed through the briars, their faces aglow with delight. Bernie followed, and Mary brought up the rear, her face as solemn as ever.

A lump rose in my throat when I saw Elena, and her eyes smiled in a way I had never seen before.

"Mr. Adams . . . Buster . . . It's good to have you back," she said, laying her slender hand on my arm.

I removed my hat and dipped my head best I could. "Mighty good to be back, Ma'am."

A hand tugged at my sleeve. I looked down into Mary's uplifted face. She opened her lips to speak, but the words failed to come. Tears welled in her eyes.

I laid my hand on hers. "You're safe, Mary. Don't worry. I won't let anything happen to you."

Elena slid her arm around Mary's shoulder and drew the solemn child into her side.

George came running up and Bernie and Rachel greeted him. The pushed and shoved each other like a litter of pups. Bernie tried to grab George's sword, but the youngster held onto it for dear life.

Bob stood behind Elena. "Everybody's okay, Mr. Adams. I kept them all safe just like you wanted."

"You did good, Bob." I laid my hand on his shoulder. "Mighty good." Then I remembered the trail they had so carefully hidden. "See any Comanches about?"

Bob and Elena glanced at each other. "Some," she replied.

"I don't know if they was Comanche or not, but we spotted some Injuns." He nodded to the underbrush behind them. "That's why we hid in this cave."

I looked at the underbrush. "Cave? What cave?"

Bernie yanked at my sleeve. "Over there, Mr. Adams. I found it."

Elena nodded. "I've never seen one like it, Buster. It must've been someone's regular home."

Bernie and Rachel had crowded in, listening to the conversation.

"It's a real nice cave, Mr. Adams. Come see," said Rachel.

"Let's get the horses first." I looked at Elena. "We didn't spot any Comanches anywhere around. How about boiling us a pot of coffee?"

Elena and the girls disappeared behind the underbrush. Bob looked at me uncomfortably, licking his lips and glancing around. "Anything wrong, Bob?"

He took a deep breath. "We lost the horses."

I looked around. "All of them?"

"Yes, sir. All of them."

"What happened?"

"It was all my fault, Mr. Adams. When I—"

"Forget about fault, Bob. Just tell me what happened."

"It was when we spotted the Injuns. I got ever'body in the cave, but I must not have tied the horses good because next morning they was gone. We didn't hear nothing, so I figured I just hadn't tied them tight enough. Coyotes must've spooked them."

Shoulders slumped, he stared at his feet. "I'm sorry, Mr. Adams. Honest."

I studied him a moment. At least, he wasn't trying to crawfish out of the blame. "Forget it, Bob. We still got the wagon and two horses, and we got our feet. Besides, San Antone is only fifteen or twenty miles. We'll be there tomorrow night."

He looked up at me and grinned. I clapped him on

the shoulder. "Now, let's us go in and get some of that coffee."

Elena and the children were right about the cave. The entrance was made up of two switchbacks, effectively preventing any fire from being spotted outside. The main room was thirty feet square, and holes had been drilled in the walls in which iron rods had been inserted to support wooden shelves, all of which were dry and rotten, falling apart at the slightest touch.

Four tunnels led from the cave. "Where do those go?" I asked.

Bob stepped forward. "We don't know, Mr. Adams. I . . . " He hesitated, drew up his shoulders, and stared me square in the eye. "I wouldn't let anyone go in there until you got back."

He stared at me, unsure of my reaction.

I grinned at him. "Smart move, Bob. Just what a man would do."

His face lit up, and he looked at Elena, pride swelling his chest almost to bursting.

"Let's have some of those candles and see where these tunnels go. No telling what we'll find back there." Each boy carried a candle as we entered the first tunnel, which led into an antechamber around the perimeter of which were several bunks, most dry-rotted. On the floor were strewn blankets that fell apart at the touch, and in one corner lay a small book, which turned to ashes wherever I touched it.

Holding the candle closer, I blew gently on the pages to remove the ashes. The words on the page appeared to be written in Spanish.

Elena whispered. "What was it, do you think?"

"Maybe a diary or a log of some sort."

The second tunnel led to another large room that opened onto a ten acre meadow, in the middle of which sparkled a small pond. Looming crags surrounded the valley. "Never find us here," I muttered.

Elena, who followed me, nodded.

The third chamber was as the first, but the fourth— the fourth chamber is where we found the gold!

At first, we thought we had found another skeleton; but when I poked it with my toe, it didn't fall apart like the one back in the other cave.

"Is it a skeleton?" asked Elena.

Beneath the cloth was a feel of something solid, not hard like a rock, but solid, with some give. I removed the cloth. "Bags," I said. "Something in them." I tried to pick up one about the size of a fruit jar, but it was too heavy. "Looks like it's made out of some kind of leather or heavy cloth."

I squatted by the bag, and the children crowded in around me. A drip of wax from George's candle fell on my neck. "Ouch," I yelled, jumping to my feet and grabbing my neck. I glared at the children, who were all staring at me wide-eyed, unaware of what had happened. "Watch those candles, you hear? That wax burns."

Bob glanced at Elena who suppressed a grin.

Maintaining my dignity, I squatted by the bag and untied the thong around the neck. I tried to open the neck, but a piece tore loose. I studied the material. It was some kind of heavy cloth.

Carefully, I worked the neck open and peered inside. Something glimmered. My heart stopped beating. I had heard about this—but—Could I be mistaken?

My fingers shook as I reached into the bag. "Get a candle down here, hurry."

George, ever near with that candle, stuck it down by the bag, narrowly missing singeing my eyebrows. I pulled my fingers from the bag. I turned my hand palm up and opened my fingers. Several glistening grains of gold fell into my palm.

Elena gasped.

"What is it?" asked Rachel.

Bob snapped, "What do you think, dummy? It's gold."

Bernie looked at me. "Gold? Really gold?"

The next thing I knew, Elena was laughing and beating me on the shoulders and neck. "It's gold, it's gold, it's gold."

Even Sally the goose got into the celebration. She flapped her wings and charged me.

Later in the main chamber, after we had all calmed

down and eaten a supper of venison and cornbread and the children had dropped off into a blissful sleep, I poured a second cup of coffee and leaned back on my saddle to study the pile of bags in the middle of the floor.

"Mary tried to speak," I said.

Elena smiled. "Yes."

"You think she's coming out of it?"

She hesitated. "Hard to say. Maybe."

I looked into the shadows of the chamber where the small girl slept, her book cradled to her cheek. "I hope so." But even if she were coming to terms with the horror of that day, the poor kid would still need a heap of patience.

Elena studied me a moment. "You're a good man, Buster."

I got nervous and changed the subject. "We need to make some new bags for the gold. Those bags there will fall to pieces when we start moving them."

Elena leaned forward. "How much is there, do you think?"

I shook my head. "Hundred pounds more or less, I'd guess. I'm not sure what gold is going for, but I'd guess we probably have us thirty to forty thousand dollars piled up there." Holding the hot tin cup with the tips of my fingers, I sipped the coffee.

She gasped and clapped her hands together. The flickering glow from the small fire bathed her face with a golden glow. She reminded me of a picture I had once seen of a nun, all soft and gentle.

Her next words cast a blur on that image. "That much money will buy a nice little ranch for the children."

The way she said *that much money* made me wonder. I honestly detest arguing with a woman. I'll do anything I can to avoid disagreement with one, but if I had to disagree, I figured now was the time to start, to let her know just where I stood on this whole matter. "Hold on there. Now, you can do anything you want with your share, but don't count on using mine."

The soft and gentle expression disappeared as if I had slapped her across the face. The image of that nun vanished in the blink of an eye. "What do you mean by that, Mr. Adams?"

Now we were back to Mr. Adams. I sipped my coffee and stared across the fire at her. "There's seven of us. I figure I deserve an equal split of the proceeds. Like I say, you six can do whatever your little hearts desire, but I'm taking my share back to Bastrop and put it into my ranch."

I heard a saying once about "hell having no fury like a woman scorned." Well, you can put *deprived of money* right up there with *scorned*.

"You mean," she began, glaring at me. "You mean you're going to take these poor children's money for yourself? I told you that day in the cave I needed money to buy up a place to take care of them so they won't have to go to the orphanage.'' She paused and glanced around at the children slumbering peacefully. ''You really want these unfortunate children to go to an orphanage.''

I squeezed the tin handle on the cup so hard, it collapsed, tilting the cup backward and spilling the hot coffee on my belly. I yelped and sat up, brushing at the steaming liquid.

She tilted her chin. ''Serves you right.''

I gave her a hard look that would have singed anyone else's head bald, but she just ignored me.

''Trying to make me feel guilty won't work, Miss Wallace. You and the children's share of this gold will be between twenty-five and thirty-five thousand. That's more than enough to set up you and the kids, to set up anybody, in a nice little ranch with plenty of working stock.''

Elena didn't respond to my last comment. Instead, she shot me a cold look, lay down with her back to me, and pulled her blanket over her shoulder.

Disgusted with the sudden turn of events, I rose and slipped outside, pausing in the shadows of the spreading post oaks. Below me, the Medina River was a silvery road twisting through the rugged countryside.

The night was silent and still except for the occasional chirrup of a cricket or the lonely howl of a coyote. The sense of awesome solitude gave a jasper reason to ponder. On the one hand, I understood Elena's desire to make sure the children were provided for, but on the other, I felt I was entitled to a share for all I had sacrificed to help them reach San Antone safely. It was almost like the good Lord was giving me another chance to save my ranch.

I thought back over the trip, the laughter, the tribulations. And for some strange reason, I thought of Cheyenne Bill Longstrum. Had he escaped the Comanches on that rain-drenched day? Or was he lying dead and scalped like so many other white men? I couldn't believe he was dead. Cheyenne Bill had more lives than a cat.

Hey nickered. "Getting restless, fella?" I whispered, patting his neck and scratching behind his ears. "We oughta reach San Antone tomorrow, and then all this will be behind us."

He shook his head.

"Reckon that'll suit you, huh?"

Again he shook his head.

I stared to the east for several moments, picturing riding up to Natalia Ludden's house on Hey, me dressed in new duds, and Hey's bridle and saddle all nice and shiny clean. Her pa would frown when he saw me, but as soon as his greedy eyes lit on my bag of gold, the frown would be replaced with a great smile.

An even wider smile curled my lips as I imagined John Chapman Ludden kow-towing to me. I'd have to think of just the right words to put him in his place, and then I'd hold out my hand to Natalia, and we would ride away to our own ranch.

"Mr. Adams?"

I jumped at the words spoken at my back. I spun around. "Who? Who's that?"

A little girl's voice spoke up from the darkness. "It's just me, Mr. Adams, Rachel Sheridan. I . . . I didn't mean to scare you."

Immediately I squinted into the darkness behind her, searching for that insane goose. "Where's Sally?"

"Oh, she's still sleeping. I didn't want to disturb her. Besides, I wanted to ask you something in secret. You don't mind, do you?"

She sounded so grave, so concerned I had to grin. "Of course not, sweetheart." I squatted in front of her. The moonlight filtering through the leaves overhead speckled her serious little face. "You can ask me anything you want."

She drew a deep breath. "D . . . Don't you like us anymore?"

Her words kicked me between my eyes. "Why, what a thing to ask, Rachel. Of course I like you kids. Why do you ask?"

She shrugged. "I don't know."

I prompted her. "You can tell me, Rachel. I'm your friend."

"Bernie said so."

"Bernie? What's Bernie got to do with it?"

Rachel hesitated, then whispered. "He said you wasn't going to live with us after we got to wherever we was going. That you was going to leave us behind."

I touched my finger to her chin. "Well, that's kinda true, but it doesn't mean I don't like you. You see, I've got my own ranch, and when I get you to San Antone, you'll have one of your own. But, I'll come back and see you. Okay?"

I felt her chin quiver, and she sniffed. "But we love you. Why can't we go with you?"

Chapter Thirteen

Well, I did what most grown-ups do at a time like that, I rambled around, giving two dozen excuses, none of which really meant anything to the little girl. By the time I asked her if she understood, I had her so confused, she just simply nodded, and without another word, returned to the cave.

Maybe I had steered her away from her question, but it loomed mighty large in my own head. I had grown attached to these youngsters. They'd all grown up, some more than others, and none of them had ever whined or cried, other than Bernie once or twice until I threatened to kick his rump.

I turned back to Hey. "Why do things get so confusing?"

Hey just looked at me.

While Elena and the children ate breakfast, I placed the gold in bags cut from the canvas top. They were not bags, but actually large squares, the perimeter of which was pulled together over the pile of gold and tied. We ended up with four bags, each one containing about twenty-five pounds.

We loaded the gold in the bottom of the *carreta*, and placed the remaining canvas over it. We pulled the donkey from the harness and fit George's mustang in its place. If we had to make a run, the pony would be superior to the donkey.

The women rode in the *carreta*. George and Bernie walked, which gave George more opportunities to slay the enemy with his sword. Bob rode drag on the donkey; I rode point.

The day was a typical late spring day. A sky as blue as a robin's egg, and not a cloud in sight. The sun was bright and warm, a portent of the heat we would be facing later in the day.

It was the kind of day I enjoyed, leaning back in the saddle and relishing the vast and glorious panorama of Texas, the rugged hills and deep canyons, the savannahs and meadows lush with bluestem and switchgrass, the streams and rivers cold and sweet.

I shook my head. No wonder back east the initials *GTT* were painted on the doors of so many vacant homesteads and businesses. A mockingbird swooped low. In the distance, a blue jay squawked angrily. Down below us, a deer looked up from watering at a small pond.

GTT. Gone to Texas. Yep, no wonder so many mothers lost their sons to the one woman no one could tame, Texas—wild, reckless, exciting, dangerous, ready to open its arms and wealth to those with the courage, strength and guts to take it.

We were skirting the edge of a large savannah. To our left, a vertical face of rocky bluffs overlooked the grassy plain. Ahead, the savannah narrowed into a slender neck between a thick brake of post oak and the escarpment. Once through the neck we would strike the San Antonio/Web Town road. From then on, we could ride into San Antone with bells ringing.

Suddenly, a gunshot broke the silence, and the pommel on my saddle disappeared. Hey jerked aside from the impact of the slug on the saddle, almost unseating me. I held tight, palming my .44 and wheeling back to the *carreta*. More shots rang out, whipping past me like angry hornets.

Elena had stopped the donkey, and I waved her into a patch of shin oak and mesquite. Slugs tore up the ground around the *carreta*, then just as abruptly, stopped.

Behind her, Bob came galloping, one elbow flapping, and his Sharps raised over his head with his other hand. He veered his pony into the shin oak patch after Elena.

Above the patch was a small bluff, no more than fifteen feet high. I rode around behind, and dismounting, quickly climbed to the top and lay behind some small boulders. Easing my Winchester forward, I looked down at the *carreta*. Elena and the girls had climbed out and were crouched against one of the large wooden wheels. Bernie and George were missing.

Before I could call out, I spotted movement in a patch of cedar a few yards beyond Elena and the children. A face looked up, and a hand waved. I sighed with relief. George and Bernie. Naturally, George had that blasted sword in his hand. I motioned for them to keep their heads down.

We waited. My eyes quartered the lay of the land before us, searching for any movement. In the distance, a thin wisp of dust rose into the air. I strained for the sound of hoof beats, but all I heard was the soft moaning of the afternoon breeze curling through the rugged countryside.

Bob looked up at me, his expression questioning our next move. I gestured for him to stay as he was.

He nodded and cocked the Sharps.

I slithered backward on my belly until I reached a small copse of cedar. I rose into a crouch and swung wide along the top of the escarpment, dodging the spindly cedar and blossoming prickly pear, planning on coming in from the rear of whoever had pulled down on us. From the slug's impact on the pommel, I knew the shot had come from the stand of cedar on the far side of the savannah.

After a mile or so, I found a shallow arroyo leading off the escarpment. I paused behind a thick patch of prickly pear and studied the open plains and the dark brake beyond. The only movement was the flittering of birds and the bobbing flight of colorful butterflies.

I measured the distance to the nearest patch of oak. Two hundred yards, at least. Taking a deep breath, I broke across the grassy plain, expecting the jolting impact of a slug with every step.

My breath came in labored gasps, but I kept my head down and my legs pumping like the wheels on those fancy 4–6–0 locomotives up around Dodge City and Wichita. Slowly, the line of cedar drew closer.

Just before I reached the thick curtain of cedars, a figure stepped from behind a tree and jerked a double barreled shotgun to his shoulder. I'd like to say I reacted instantly, but what really saved my hide was a root I stubbed my toe on, sending me stumbling to the ground.

My attacker touched off one shot that tore a chunk out of the brim on the back of my hat. While I was tumbling head over heels, he fired the other barrel, tearing up a handful of ground beside me. I rolled onto my belly and snapped off two fast shots, but he had already bolted back into the cedars, zigzagging between the trees to present a more difficult target.

Suddenly, shots sounded back in the canyon. The boom of the Sharps rolled across the savannah.

I threw the fleeing killer a last glance, then raced back to the canyon, the mouth of which was at least a mile distant.

Abruptly, the firing ceased. A moment later, four riders and the *carreta*, with my horse tied behind, burst from the canyon, cutting directly toward me.

As soon as the riders saw me, they began firing. One of the disadvantages of the handgun is its appalling inaccuracy from the back of a galloping horse, so I wasn't too concerned about kneeling out there in the open and drawing down on the approaching riders with my Winchester.

I grimaced. The *carreta*, loaded with Elena and the children, was behind the riders. I couldn't take a chance on a wild slug striking the cart.

I broke toward the escarpment, hoping to at least get one or two shots from the side, but as if reading my mind, the riders dropped back to surround the *carreta*. I muttered a dark curse.

The rider in front waved at me and laughed. Cheyenne Bill Longstrum. I muttered a darker curse and fell to the ground as they threw half-a-dozen wild slugs in my direction.

Peering over the switchgrass and bluestem, I tried to

make out the heads bobbing up and down in the *carreta*, but at such a distance, they all blurred together.

Behind me, the donkey brayed.

For a moment, I considered leaving the donkey. I could make better time on foot, and she could take care of herself out here. She brayed again. I wondered if she had been shot.

If she were badly injured, I wouldn't want her to just lie there and suffer. Better to put the unfortunate animal out of her misery than let the coyotes and wolves tear into her while she still lived.

But the donkey had not been scratched. She stood near a patch of lush browse, chewing awhile, then braying awhile. I reckon she was as close to heaven as donkeys ever get.

I approached her and laid my hand on her neck. "What's the matter, little one. They go off and leave you?"

"Pssst! Mr. Adams!"

I spun and dropped to one knee. My sixgun appeared in my hand like magic.

"Mr. Adams. It's me, George."

My heart pounded in my chest. Had he been hurt so badly they just left him? "Where are you, boy?"

A patch of cedar moved. "Over here." The limbs parted, and he tip-toed out, sword in hand. "Have they gone?"

I stared at him in disbelief. "What are you doing here?"

He looked around, and when he was satisfied that we were alone, he grinned up at me. "I hid real good. The outlaws didn't even look for me."

That didn't make sense. "Why not?"

"When they asked Elena if they had all the children, she said yes—but she knew I was hiding in the cedar. She saw me."

Nodding, I fit the picture together. "Everybody all right? No one hurt?"

"No, sir. Bob, they took his rifle, but he's okay."

I holstered my handgun. "Well, you feel up to traveling, boy? Let's go. We got to find them."

George slipped his sword under his belt. "Oh, that won't be hard, Mr. Adams."

"What?" I frowned at him, irritated. "You don't know what you're talking about. They got horses, and we're on foot."

"Yes, sir, I know, but they said they was going to a place called Web Town. I think that's what they called it."

I grabbed his shoulder. "Web Town? Are you sure, boy? Are you sure?"

He squirmed under my grasp. "Oh, that hurts, Mr. Adams."

Quickly I released him. "Sorry, boy, but are you sure? They did say Web Town?"

He nodded emphatically. "Yes, sir. The big one who has the feather in his hat. He said it."

I grunted. "Cheyenne Bill," I mumbled.

"What did you say, Mr. Adams?"

"Nothing, boy, nothing."

A cold wind chilled me as I looked to the northeast in the direction of Web Town, a shanty town made up of drunks and outlaws, wild women and desperate men, thieves and swindlers.

I had ridden through Web Town on two or three occasions, never stopping. The ramshackle buildings and muddy streets reeked of filth. If there had ever been a city on the face of the earth that deserved to be destroyed, Web Town was it.

"How are you on running, George?" I pulled off my boots and using the butt of my sixgun, knocked the heels off.

"Okay, I guess." He watched me curiously. "Why?"

"You and me, we got some running to do." I pointed to the northeast, over the rugged crags choked with oak and cedar. "Web Town's yonder. We're cutting across, hoping to reach the town before they do. It's a mighty bad place to put women and children."

I started to say more, but decided to hold my silence. The boy didn't need to know that Web Town was the meeting place of Comancheros, men who purchased women and children for resale down in Mexico to wealthy landowners and Apaches.

George nodded to the donkey. "What about her? You can't just leave her out here."

"Don't worry about her, son. Out here will be like a Garden of Eden compared to the life she's had."

He pointed behind me. "What about her?"

I looked around and stared right into the beady eyes of Sally the goose. I shook my head. "What about her?"

"We can't leave her out here. What will Rachel do if Sally gets hurt?"

"No." I shook my head. "No. I'm not taking that goose. She can stay around here, and we'll come back and get her. Okay?"

He looked at me, disappointed.

I shrugged.

Best I could remember, the Web Town road was still five or six miles distant, and from there, Cheyenne Bill had another ten north to the shabby little village. I could save four or five miles by cutting across.

We moved out, clambering over the first ridge of rocky outcroppings before dropping into a valley, which we covered in a loping trot. I kept my pace slow so as not to wear out George, but if I were really honest, I'd admit that I kept it slow for me as much as for him.

When we had covered about two miles, George yelled. "Look. Back there. It's Sally."

I looked back, and sure enough, waddling and flying

and quacking in an effort to keep up with us was the goose. I shook my head and stared into the heavens, wondering just what I had done to deserve all this good luck.

The sun baked the countryside. We had four hours until dark, and I knew there was no way we could cover eleven or so miles in four hours.

Even if darkness caught Cheyenne Bill, they could keep moving. I shook my head and pushed on, clenching my teeth. I'd get Elena and those kids back if I had to tear that dirty little town apart.

We were still four or five miles from the town at sunset.

"Let's pull up here for a few minutes and rest, George."

The young boy looked up at me, his face pale and drawn, his torn clothes clinging to his thin body. "I ain't tired, Mr. Adams."

"I know, but we best not travel until we get a moon. No sense in taking a chance on breaking a leg or anything."

He didn't argue. He sagged to the ground like a wet rag, and in the next breath, he was asleep.

I studied the young feller. Quite a kid. Quite a kid.

Looking over my shoulder, I spotted Sally standing quietly about forty yards away.

Chapter Fourteen

We moved out at moonrise. At two o'clock, we topped out on a hill overlooking Web Town. The town lay dark and silent in the cold light of the moon, its sagging buildings leaning against each other for support like a roomful of drunks.

I didn't have any idea where Sally was, but I left George on the outskirts of town, hidden in a safe niche between two boulders behind a stand of cedar. "Don't go to sleep on me. You hear me whistle, be ready to run."

He pulled his sword. "Don't worry about me. I can take care of myself."

I mussed his hair and grinned. "I reckon you can, boy. I reckon you can."

Leaving George behind, I slipped into town, hiding in the shadows of the first structure, a rickety building that was a saloon from the smell of it. Dropping into a crouch, I slipped up to the corner of the saloon and studied the darkness before me. I was looking for the *carreta*. They could hide their horses, but a cumbersome wagon with five foot wooden wheels was mighty hard to conceal.

Three more sagging structures were to my left, and across the street squatted three more. Behind the three, the moonlight touched on a wagon. I craned my neck for a better view, but the shadows and the dim light created distorted images.

I had to get closer, but I dared not chance crossing the moonlit street. Drawing back, I disappeared into the darkness behind the saloon. Moving silently, I made my way back to George, and then swung wide, staying in the shadows of the trees until I came up behind what appeared to be a barn.

I froze. In front of the barn sat the *carreta* next to a buckboard. Behind the barn, several horses milled about in the corral. My pulse raced. Elena and the children must be in the barn, if—I clenched my teeth, hoping they were all unharmed. If those scum had laid a hand on Elena or the children, I'd—

Taking a deep breath, I stared at the brilliant stars overhead, trying to control my anger. There were at least four owlhoots, maybe more. Before I went storming in, I had to know what I was facing.

I crouched in the darkness behind a cedar and watched the barn. No movement.

The minutes dragged into an hour. From the position of the Big Dipper, I figured the time to be around five o'clock, not long 'til sunrise. I grimaced. I was running out of time if I was going to take them tonight. And I didn't see where I had a choice. For all I knew, come morning, they might be sold to a handful of different buyers.

My break came when a cowpoke staggered from the barn, scrubbing his eyes with his fists. I moved fast, ghosting to the corner of the barn. The cowpoke paused and stretched, his back to me. The barn door was open, the gaping mouth a black hole in the silvery night.

I had made and discarded several plans. The sobering truth was that until I knew exactly where Elena and the children were, I could do nothing. I glanced over my shoulder. At any moment, the sky would begin to gray.

Taking a deep breath, I eased along the front of the barn to the open door, keeping eyes on the jasper with his back to me. Without hesitation, I slipped around the door and pressed up against the wall in the darkness, my ears straining to pick up any indication I had been spotted. Nothing.

Nerves on edge, I eased along the wall, grateful for

the hay under my feet. I encountered a wall. I ran my fingers up the wall. I touched a trace chain. Next to the chain hung leather reins. To the left of the reins was an opening in the wall. A stall. Leaning forward, I tried to pick up any animal sounds, but the stall was as silent as the rest of the barn. Moving carefully, I edged into the opening and crouched, putting the wall between me and the rest of the barn.

Moments later, the cowboy entered the barn, and I heard the rusty squeak of a barn lamp being opened. A weak, yellow light pushed back the darkness in the middle of the barn.

"Rise an' shine, boys. Time to be moving on."

Two or three voices mumbled, followed by the sound of stirring bodies and sleepy oaths.

Rising to my feet, I peered over the top of the stall, the hanging bridles and harnesses throwing shadows across my face. Quickly, I scanned the barn. All I saw were three men.

Elena and the children were missing!

"What about the woman and kids?" mumbled one of the cowpokes, scratching his head and yawning.

"Still sleeping, I reckon," replied another, taking the lantern and crossing the barn to another stall. He stuck the lantern inside and grunted. "Well, missy, you look like you ain't had much sleep."

A feminine voice replied, but it was too faint for me to make out.

The yawning cowboy barked. "Leave that female alone, Gus. You hurt her, and Bill'll throw you to the Comanche."

Gus shrugged and returned to the middle of the barn and reached for his boots. He rolled his shoulders. "I still don't know why we couldn't of slept inside like Bill. I got me a blasted crick in my neck."

The other cowpoke nodded to a small pile under a blanket. "The gold, you dumb hammerhead. Bill didn't want them others in the house to know we got it. We'll just load it back in the cart nice and quiet-like, and pull out."

Gus yanked on his boot. "Well, I still woulda preferred the house. We could of gone inside when the others rode out just after midnight. Bill didn't have no right keeping us out here."

I eased the muzzle of my .44 through the tangle of harness and cocked the hammer. All three froze at the crisp click of the hammer. "That's right, boys. Put those hands up and pretend you're a rock, and don't move."

They did as I said.

They were all right handers. "Take your left hand and drop your gunbelt. Now." I snapped, my voice low.

Again they did as I said.

"Who are you, mister? You trying to hold us up, you're in big trouble."

"Shut up," I replied, my voice low and guttural. "You want a hole in your forehead to match that one above your chin, just keep talking."

He clamped his mouth shut.

"Okay. You two there, on the right. Lay on your bellies and put your hands behind your back. And you, Gus. Get that lariat off that saddle and tie 'em good and snug."

He attempted to leave some slack between the wrists, but I spotted it. "Okay now, Gus, just you throw a couple loops around those wrists and snug 'em up just like you was tying down a calf. You don't, and I'll see you never have a second chance to test your mettle as a calf roper."

I remained in the shadows, but he recognized the promise in my voice. He obeyed, snugging the ropes so tight they cut into his compadres' flesh.

"That's good, Gus," I said, stepping into the light.

His eyebrows lifted in surprise when he saw me. I sounded a lot bigger than I am, and when he saw a feller about six inches shorter than him come out of the shadows, he felt a little foolish. His muscles tensed.

I tilted the muzzle of the .44. "Don't try it, Gus. Mr. Colt, he made us small ones just as big as you." I took a step toward him. "Now, you lay down."

He took a step backward and rolled his muscular shoulders. "You ain't goin' to shoot. You'll wake up them in the house."

"Maybe so, but you won't be around to see them," I replied, noting how he was leaning forward and doubling his big fists. "Just do like I said. Hit the ground."

He studied me for several seconds. I could see the wheels turning in his head. Could he reach me before I got off a shot? Would I even shoot? Excitement and fear flushed his face.

Dropping his shoulders, he stooped to the ground, but in the next instant, he charged me, bellowing like a bull, his massive arms flailing like a machine.

I side-stepped and whopped him across the back of his head with the muzzle of my sixgun. He fell like a pole-axed steer.

Holstering my handgun, I quickly tied him hand and foot, and gagged all three men. Then I grabbed the lantern and hurried to the stall.

Elena was sitting up, her face filled with hope. I hooked the lantern over a nail and quickly untied her. "Hurry," I whispered. "Untie the kids while I saddle some horses."

She grabbed my hand. "No, Buster. The cart. We've got to take the gold with us."

I glared at her. "You're crazy."

"Please. The children."

I couldn't afford to argue with her any longer, and then I remembered the buckboard outside. I nodded. "Okay. Hurry."

Rising to my feet, I grabbed the harness and headed

for the back door and the corral. Just as I reached it, the door opened and Cheyenne Bill Longstrum stood grinning at me, a sixgun in his hand.

I dropped the harness and froze, my fingers inches from the butt of my .44.

His grin grew wider into a lop-sided, gap-toothed leer. "Well, well, well. My old friend, Buster Adams. You surprised me. I didn't figure you'd get here so fast, but that makes no never mind. Not now, it don't." He glanced at his trussed-up gunhands. "Dependable help's hard to find nowadays."

Behind me, Elena gasped.

The sneer on Bill's face twisted into an expression of pure hatred when he saw her, when he realized just how close we had come to escaping. He looked back at me, his eyes dark slits. "You . . ."

For several seconds, Cheyenne Bill stared at me, his entire body trembling in anger. Slowly, the anger cooled, and he plastered a crooked grin back on his face. "You sure don't waste no time, Buster. Well, I don't waste no time either. You ain't goin' to bother me no more."

He cocked his handgun.

I knew I was going to catch some lead. I couldn't jump aside because Elena and the kids were behind me. My only chance was that he would not hit a vital spot.

"Adios, Buster. It's been—Owwww . . ." He

leaped forward, his arms splayed wide, his sixgun firing into the ceiling.

Never one to turn down a free drink or miss an opportunity, I stepped forward and drove my fist into his jaw. He came to an instant standstill, his eyes glazed, his mouth open. Old Bill tried to say something, but his eyes just rolled up in his head, and he collapsed to the ground.

Behind him stood Sally the goose and George, his sword held high. On the tip of the rapier was blood, blood from Cheyenne Bill Longstrum's rump.

I just stared at the boy. He had a grin on his face wide enough to cross the Medina River. The smile faded into a frown. "Are you mad at me, Mr. Adams?"

"Me? Why should I be mad at you, George?"

"I didn't do what you told me. I didn't stay hid out."

It was my turn to grin. "Boy, you just keep disobeying me like that from now on, and you and me'll get along just fine."

Elena laughed and hugged George. Rachel scrambled to Sally, and the others, even Mary, clustered around George just like he was a big chocolate cake, all of them jabbering at once and no one understanding a single thing they said.

"Hold on, there," I called out. "We still got to get out of here." I picked up the harness. "Bob, you tie Bill up. Tie him snug and tight. George, bring us a horse for the buckboard. The rest of you, pick up that gold and stack it in the back of the buckboard.''

The buckboard had butcher-knife wheels. Once we hit the road, we could make good time, but that meant we were in for a rough ride. Luckily for Elena, who would be driving, the seat had springs. She would bounce, but not like the children in the back of the buckboard.

While they finished stacking the gold under the seat, I found Hey in the corral and saddled him.

Back in the barn, I checked the outlaws' bonds. Gus and Bill were still unconscious. One of the other two craned his neck to look up at me. ''You'd better skedaddle. Soon as we're loose, we're coming after you.''

I stared down at him, considering his words. Nodding, I dropped Hey's reins, returned to the corral, threw open the gate, and stampeded the horses into the surrounding countryside.

Back in the barn, I nodded to him. ''Have at it.''

Chapter Fifteen

As soon as we got out of town, Elena started to lay the whip to the blue roan I had harnessed to the buckboard.

"Not yet," I said, stopping her.

She looked at me quizzically.

I explained. "We got twenty miles to San Antone. Four hours at a nice trot. If we try to make it in two, we won't get ten miles."

Bob, who sat on the seat with Elena, pointed to the barn. "What about them? They're going to get loose sooner or later, and you know they're coming after this gold."

"Can't be helped," I replied, shrugging. "We kill this horse, they'll get us for sure."

175

Bob cast a worried glance back at the barn. I didn't blame him. I was worried too, but I had made up my mind that one way or another, I would get Elena and these children to San Antone. I had given up way too much not to.

The sun had risen, and the day promised to be special, blue skies, puffy clouds, but I didn't pay it much attention. I should have, for more times than not, when things look rosy and pretty for me, they turn out black and ugly. I had too much else on my mind right then.

As we rode, I pulled a box of .44 cartridges from my saddlebags and replenished the empty loops in my gunbelt and made sure both my Winchester and handgun were fully loaded.

Bob saw me and double-checked his Sharps.

We were an odd-looking lot, a down-at-the-heels cowpoke followed by a woman, five children, and one goose in a buckboard.

I kept looking over my shoulder.

By mid-morning, strong gusts of gulf winds pushed dark clouds over the horizon. Rumbles of thunder rolled across the undulating prairie before us.

We met two or three other travelers, Mexican peons taking produce to market. They plodded along, moving aside so we could pass.

Pulling up beside an old peon, I asked. *"¿A qué distancia a San Antonio, gusta?"*

He smiled broadly and held up his hand and spread his fingers. *"Cinco millas, señor."*

"Gracias."

"Eres de nada, señor."

I relaxed. We were close. Only five miles. Just another hour.

I had turned to give Elena and the children the good news when I heard the hoofbeats. Even before I looked, I knew who was responsible.

A single glance confirmed my fears. Four riders were coming fast.

"Let's raise some dust," I yelled, whipping off my hat and slamming it on the blue roan's rump.

Elena popped the reins, and the roan broke into a gallop. The children lay in the bed of the buckboard. Gun in hand, I brought up the rear.

Longstrum and his gunnies were still a half mile behind, but they would catch us long before we reached San Antone. Our best bet was to try to get a couple miles closer to town before making our stand.

After a mile, they had closed within a quarter-of-a-mile. I holstered my handgun and pulled out the Winchester. At such a distance, the slug would drop several feet, but if I could kick up some dust in the road ahead of them, they might slow enough for us to pick up some more time.

I aimed a couple feet over their heads. The slug

kicked up a chunk of dirt in front of them, causing their horses to swerve. I grinned.

My humor was short-lived, for they didn't slow a step. Ahead, the road curved to the left for the last run into San Antone, three miles of small hills.

I rode up beside Elena. "Keep going," I yelled, waving to the village ahead. "Get to town." By now, the dark clouds had swept over us and ahead was a gray sheet of rain.

She nodded her understanding. I reined Hey around and dismounted, grabbing my Winchester and ducking behind a mesquite.

Two of the riders, one being Longstrum himself, veered off the road, planning on cutting across the prairie and intercepting Elena and the children. Gus and one other outlaw bore down on me.

Casting one last hurried glance at Longstrum, I jammed the Winchester into my shoulder and placed the bead in the middle of one of the riders' chest. I didn't have time to waste.

The wind gust, swirling dust and sand in my eyes, and the chill wind ahead of the rain swept over me.

Just before I fired, both riders leaned forward over their ponies' necks and began firing. I still had a shot, but now their lower profiles made it much more difficult.

As they drew closer, I placed the front bead on Gus's shoulder and squeezed off a shot.

His entire right side jerked up like a rag doll. He sprawled back across the pony's neck, and took a head first tumble to the ground.

The second rider kept pumping wild slug after wild slug.

Suddenly, he sat up in his saddle and reached for his saddlegun. I fired. My slug caught him in the chest and knocked him out of the saddle.

Without waiting to see if they were dead or alive, I jumped on Hey and headed after the buckboard. At the same time, the rain struck, a solid wall of water driven by a powerful wind.

Ahead of me, shots rang out, in the midst of the rainstorm sounding like a string of firecrackers on the Fourth of July. In the middle of the tiny pops came the boom of the Sharps.

A bolt of lightning crashed, followed by a roll of thunder.

I leaned over Hey's neck. "Let's go, boy. Don't hold back on me now."

Suddenly, I flashed past a body in the mud. I missed the face, but it was a man full-grown, not one of the children.

The Sharps boomed again, followed by two quick reports, then silence.

Hey raced sure-footed through the mud, coating me and his own chest and shoulders with a thick layer that the driving rain immediately washed away. Water was coursing across the road, runoff from the numerous hills on either side of the muddy road.

Ahead, I spotted the buckboard. My heart pounded against my chest. The buckboard had overturned. Next to it stood Bill Longstrum's horse.

A crash of lightning exploded nearby, prickling my skin and setting my hair on end. I whispered a short prayer and unleathered my .44.

Leaping from Hey before he stopped skidding, I raced to Bob who was standing clutching his arm. The other children were nearby. None seemed hurt.

"Elena? Where's Elena?" I yelled above the thunder and rain.

Bob pointed into a rocky wash. "There. She's down there. Longstrum went after her."

More water poured down the surrounding hills, running together across the road, and flooding down the wash. I stumbled and splashed through the water to where it slammed into a deep arroyo, swirling and boiling about my knees.

Elena screamed. I spun, my sixgun cocked and ready.

"Drop it, Buster," yelled Cheyenne Bill, his arm around Elena's waist and his handgun to her head. "Drop it, or I'll blow a hole in her purty head big enough to drive a wagon through."

I measured the distance between us. Fifteen feet. Too far in knee-deep water.

Bill called out again. "You heard me. I said, *drop it*!"

"Don't do it, Buster. He'll kill you."

Thunder rumbled, and a bolt of lightning streaked across the sky in a yellow arch. I saw the hate on Longstrum's face. He wasn't kidding. He'd kill her with no more compunction than he would squash a cockroach under his foot.

I held up my hand. "Let her go, Bill, and I'll drop it."

He shook his head. "You drop it now, right now, or she's dead."

Elena screamed. "Don't, Buster! Don't!"

"No choice. I got no choice," I yelled back, holding my arm out to the side and dropping my .44 into the muddy water rushing around my legs.

Bill Longstrum laughed and levelled his sixgun on me. "Now, it's your time, Buster."

"No," screamed Elena, slapping his hand down and raking her fingernails across his face.

His sixgun exploded, and a powerful force struck my left arm, spinning me around into the churning floodwaters. Muddy water poured down my throat. I coughed and gagged, but pushed myself to my feet and staggered toward Bill.

Elena was screaming and clawing at the outlaw. Bill stumbled backward, his arms crossed in front of him to ward off the suddenness and intensity of her blows. Abruptly, he struck out, backhanding her.

I grabbed his arm and spun him around, throwing a left at him. The pain in my arm exploded in my head, filling it with exploding rockets. I grimaced and grabbed my arm.

Bill cursed, and a knotted fist bounced off my forehead. He laughed, but before he had a chance to laugh a second time, I drove a hard right into his stomach.

His eyes bugged out in surprise, and he bent over in pain, gasping for breath. Putting every ounce of strength I had into a final blow, I ripped a right uppercut from my knees. I felt his nose break and his cheekbone bend.

The blow knocked him backward, and he sprawled into the flooding water and sank. I staggered after Bill, but the currents pushed him ahead of me. Once or twice, I glimpsed his tumbling body surface and then disappear.

By now, the floodwater had reached my waist. I struggled back to Elena, and together, we fought our way through the flooding arroyo to another wash up which we climbed on hands and knees.

I couldn't get Bill Longstrum out of my head. He was a tough jasper, and until I saw his dead body, I could not rest easy.

Elena and me held each other up and staggered back to the wagon against which the children had huddled.

Bob was the first to see us coming. He raced to our side, but just before he reached us, he slid to a halt, staring in disbelief over my shoulder.

Without hesitation, I shoved Elena aside and yanked the Sharps from Bob and dropped into a crouch, cocking and firing from my hip.

Cheyenne Bill Longstrum stared at me in surprise, a neat hole in his forehead, but the back of his skull blowed away. His eyes still open, he stood for another second, then crumpled to the ground.

To the south, a strip of blue showed beyond the clouds, and the rain began tapering off. I stumbled over to Bill and stared down at him.

Elena came to my side, her fingers gently touching my wounded arm. "Come to the wagon. Let me bandage your arm."

She led me back to the wagon.

I pulled up and stared at the overturned buckboard. "The gold? Where's the gold?"

We had all forgotten about it, but now we scrambled around trying to find it.

"Look," said Bob, holding up a square of canvas in which the gold had been tied. Two bullet holes had punctured the square.

George found another, and Bernie, another.

Rachel found the fourth square, but there were no holes in it.

We stared at the pieces of canvas in disbelief.

"What . . . What happened?" asked Bob.

"Those," I said, pointing to the three with holes in them. "The gold must have poured out while we were running from Longstrum. The other one must have busted loose when the buckboard overturned."

Elena looked up at me. "So the gold . . . " She couldn't complete her question.

I nodded slowly and pointed to the water still running across the road and down the wash. "The gold is out there," I said, pointing to the flooding arroyo.

Everyone, except Mary, stared at the muddy waters coursing down the arroyo. She was staring at me.

I felt it building deep inside, one of the biggest, most hysterical laughs I had ever had. Talk about nature playing tricks. This was one of the slickest.

So, I laughed.

They looked at me like I was crazy.

Then Elena understood, and she laughed, and finally, one by one, the children rolled in convulsions of laughter.

Her eyes wide with disbelief, Mary looked on as we laughed hysterically. Slowly, a faint smile erased the gloomy frown from her face. And then she laughed with us.

That night, Elena and I sat in front of a small fire in a tiny inn. The children slept on the floor around us. I had used my last few dollars to put us up. In the morning, we had to find other quarters, or make other plans.

Finally, we both drifted off.

The next morning, we loaded the children into the buckboard. I looked at Elena. "I been thinking. You want someplace for the children, and I got me a ranch. Nothing special, but it's mine, and it's paid for." I hooked my thumb over my shoulder. "It's about sixty or seventy miles thataway. If you've a mind, we can—"

A familiar voice interrupted me. "Buster! Buster Adams, you old cow thief."

I looked around to see Lorenzo Scott, my compadre who offered me the partnership on his cattle drive, dismount. He grabbed my hand and shook it roughly.

"I've been dropping around from time to time, hoping you'd made it in. Me and the boys got a thousand head of stringy longhorns about ten miles west of here, and we're headed for Abilene. You ready to go?"

To my surprise, I didn't even have to think twice. I looked back at Elena, whose face was tight with concern. "No, thanks, partner. I believe I got me a previous agreement with a hardheaded little lady, five children, and one goose." I turned to Elena. "Don't I?"

The concern vanished from her face. She shrugged and turned up her nose. "I thought you had a girl."

I read the mocking expression in her eyes. "Well, I did have a girl, but I'd rather have a woman."

Elena beamed, and the children grinned, and Sally picked that time to bite me again.

1	16
2	17
3	18
4	19
5	20
6	21
7	22
8	23
9	24
10	25
11	26
12	27
13	28
14	29
15	30
1S	4S
2S	5S
3S	6S